A SPRINKLE OF FRIENDSHIP

A SPRINKLE OF FRIENDSHIP

Coco Simon

Simon Spotlight
New York London Toronto Sydney New Delhi

This book is a work of fiction. Any references to historical events, real people, or real places are used fictitiously. Other names, characters, places, and events are products of the author's imagination, and any resemblance to actual events or places or persons, living or dead, is entirely coincidental.

SIMON SPOTLIGHT
An imprint of Simon & Schuster Children's Publishing Division
1230 Avenue of the Americas, New York, New York 10020
This Simon Spotlight edition May 2020

For information about special discounts for bulk purchases, please contact Simon & Schuster Special Sales at 1-866-506-1949 or business@simonandschuster.com.
Text by Elizabeth Doyle Carey
Jacket illustrations by Alisa Coburn
Jacket design by Alisa Coburn and Hannah Frece
Interior design by Hannah Frece
The text of this book was set in Bembo Std.
Manufactured in the United States of America 0320 FFG
10 9 8 7 6 5 4 3 2 1
ISBN 978-1-5344-6561-9 (hc)
ISBN 978-1-5344-6560-2 (pbk)
ISBN 978-1-5344-6562-6 (eBook)
Library of Congress Catalog Card Number 2020930403

CHAPTER ONE

THE LAST SPRINKLE SUNDAY BEFORE TOKYO!

"Okay, Sprinkle Sundays sisters, are you ready?"

My besties, Tamiko and Sierra, each gave a thumbs-up from behind the counter. I switched the sign on the front door from CLOSED to OPEN. "Ta-da! Molly's is open for another beautiful summer day!"

It was a Sunday afternoon, and Tamiko, Sierra, and I were working our usual shift at my mom's ice cream parlor, Molly's. The bell on the door jingled as our first customers of the day entered the store.

"Let the post-day-camp games begin!" joked Tamiko, while Sierra greeted a mom and two sweaty and tired-looking little boys wearing camp T-shirts.

"Hey, I went to Whalers Camp when I was your age!" said Sierra to the boys, and suddenly they weren't tired at all but were chatting enthusiastically to Sierra about Spikeball tournaments and swim races and skippers-versus-captains team competitions.

Tamiko laughed and shook her head. "I don't know how she does it!"

"What?" I asked, though I was pretty sure I knew what she meant.

"Sierra charms everyone! That girl can't go five minutes without making a new friend!"

I watched as Sierra gave the boys their ice creams and then showed off a complicated Whalers Camp high-five handshake that left them all laughing. "Yeah," I said. "She's living proof of that saying 'A stranger is just a friend you haven't met yet.' I can't relate! I'd pretty much always rather be reading a book instead."

"I agree. Who wants to waste energy on people you don't even know, who might be annoying anyway?"

"Tamiko!" I had to smile because she was so outrageous sometimes. "That's not nice!"

Tamiko shrugged. "I just can't pretend to be interested. Anyway, I already have enough friends."

"But, Tamiko, how can you talk about not needing new friends? You've made all those new friends at the Y!"

With school out for the past month, each of us had done different things. I had gone back up to my old camp, Holly Oaks in New Hampshire, for three awesome weeks of cool weather, arts and crafts, and swimming in the crystal clear lake. I had a bunch of old friends there from when I was little, and I just relaxed and didn't have to worry about my social life. Unlike here at home, where I'd had to move and leave my besties, Tamiko and Sierra, at my old school without me (*and* I'd had to try to make friends at my new school) . . . all because of my parents' divorce.

For the previous five years, I'd gone to camp for the whole summer, and I'd adored it. This year, our budget had only allowed for a half session at Holly Oaks camp. But as consolation, my parents had let me sign up for a food-writing class for kids at the Y here in Bayville, which started tomorrow. I loved reading and writing and food, so I was excited to combine all three in one class, even though I was nervous about meeting new kids again. Despite what Tamiko had said, she was actually pretty good in the friend-making department, while I was shy.

"Blah, blah, blah," said Tamiko. "That doesn't count. Those kids and I share interests, like colleagues, so it's more like networking. We're all artistic and creative, and we all have blogs and portfolios that we help one another with. We have a lot in common. I don't just bond with random strangers all over the place, like this one!" She jerked her thumb at Sierra, who had sent the happy customers on their way and joined our conversation.

"What? I'm not bonding with random strangers! Those kids go to my camp!"

Tamiko and I looked at each other, and we both rolled our eyes. "You could find common ground with anyone, Sierra," said Tamiko. "It just comes easily to you. Look at all the new friends you've made this year! No rhyme or reason."

Sierra bristled. "That's not true! MacKenzie is in my science class. The girls from my band are . . . in my band. The student council kids . . . Well, forget about them. The kids from soccer and softball—we have our teams in common."

"Right, but what about Jenna, who you met at the park; and Sweeney, your 'cat-sitting' friend; and Philip from the pet food store?"

Sierra just shrugged and shook her head. "What can I say? I'm a people person!"

"And don't forget all her rock-band camp friends!" I added quietly.

Sierra and the rest of her band, the Wildflowers, had attended a local rock-band camp this summer. Since I'd been back for a week, I'd noticed that all the kids from the program had been stopping by the store and trying out songs for one another. My mom had even let Sierra play Wildflowers songs on the store's sound system once she'd approved them. Molly's Ice Cream was suddenly getting a reputation as a talent incubator for local bands, and I wasn't quite sure I liked it. I had wanted the store to be more of a literary ice cream parlor, and had even introduced a few bookish traditions early on, like book and ice cream pairings, that had kind of fallen by the wayside.

"Oh, well, the rock-bank camp kids are such a great group of people, and we have so much fun together! I always learn something new from each of them. For example, one of them just did a Kickstarter campaign—"

Tamiko did a facepalm and shook her head. "I'm so sorry I have to leave you to deal with this crazy socialite by yourself while I'm away, Alley Cat!"

Sierra just grinned and shook her head at us.

Tamiko and her family were leaving the next day for their vacation in Japan. I was dreading her departure, since she was so much fun and the three of us were so well balanced as a work team and best-friend group. It was funny, but I almost felt nervous about it being just Sierra and me alone. Tamiko had a way of speaking the truth, clearing the air, and calling us on any silliness, and she always kept everything running smoothly.

Plus, I didn't have a ton of friends, so with Tamiko away, 50 percent of my best friends would be gone.

I guessed Sierra felt sad about it too, because she moaned, "It's not going to be the same without you here, Tamiko!"

Tamiko sighed dramatically. "I'm going to Japan, not another planet," she said. "And it's only for three weeks. We'll keep in touch via SuperSnap, and we can even FacePage if you want. Instead of being sad, think of all the cool souvenirs I'm going to bring you back from Tokyo. You know, in Japan it's a tradition for businesspeople to bring souvenirs—usually food—back for their coworkers when they go on business trips."

My mom had just come into the front of the store from her office. She heard us chatting and said, "And all the ice cream research you're going to do for me makes this kind of like a business trip!"

"Mmm! I can't wait!" said Tamiko, patting her stomach.

My mother had given Tamiko fifty dollars to spend on researching the "soft cream" flavors in Japan. Soft cream was like our soft-serve ice cream—and it was popular for its unusual regional flavors, like soy sauce or yam or corn. Since my mom was always looking for new ideas to keep things at Molly's exciting, and since Tamiko was such a good trend-spotter, we had high hopes for Tamiko's post-trip recommendations.

"We can't wait to hear what you find. Check in often and hurry back!" I said wistfully.

"We're all going to miss you, Tamiko, but hopefully we won't have much time to be sad," my mom said.

We all looked at her, confused.

"It's summer! Ice cream season!" she reminded us. "We'll be so busy, the time will go by like that." She snapped her fingers for emphasis.

I nodded. "That's true. Hopefully we'll blink, and—presto!—Tamiko will be back."

Tamiko made a fake-annoyed face. "Well, you can miss me *a little*," she said, and everyone laughed.

Then the post-lunch crowd started to roll in and we got busy.

Besides a steady stream of day campers, a number of Sierra's music friends came in, including one of her bandmates, Tessa, who made me a little nervous. She had a crush on my good friend Colin from my new school, and . . . so did I, I guess. I made myself busy with another kind of crush while Tessa was there—crushing toppings at the back counter (okay, hiding) while Sierra chatted with her.

I caught the name "Colin," and my ears perked up. I felt myself blushing a little bit.

". . . haven't seen him much at all," Sierra was saying.

My blood boiled a little bit. It was true that he hadn't visited Molly's since I'd returned from camp, but I didn't want Tessa to know that.

"Me neither," Tessa said.

Well, that was good anyway. If I wasn't seeing him, at least *she* wasn't either.

Sierra and Tessa chatted about new lyrics for a song they were both struggling to finish. I heard the bell jingle, and a bunch of Tamiko's photography "friends" (colleagues?) came in. I sighed and let her handle their orders while I cleaned and prepped. If things got crazy—which they would, shortly—I'd rejoin the fray and take orders. For now, I preferred to stay in the background and feel sorry for myself about not having a lot of friends who could visit me at work.

After a little while, Tamiko called, "Allie! Rush! All hands on deck!"

I washed up and joined the girls at the counter. There was a line almost out the door, and I'd been so lost in my own world that I hadn't even noticed!

By the time things settled down, almost an hour and a half had passed. We'd been so busy, I hadn't even had time to look at the clock. *Gosh,* I thought. How were Sierra and I going to handle these crowds when it was only the two of us? Maybe things really *would* be so crazy with Tamiko gone that the time would fly.

Later, as we cleaned up the mess we'd made during the rush, Sierra began singing her new Wildflowers song. It was all about loving someone she hadn't even met yet. Only Sierra!

I couldn't help but laugh. "Sierra, you are so funny!

You love meeting people so much that your songs are about loving people you haven't even met yet!"

"Well, hey, it's true! All our future boyfriends are out there somewhere right now!"

Tamiko folded her hands and put them to her cheek in a fake-dreamy pose. "Yes, and mine's so busy inventing a new social media app that will take the world by storm, he has no time to meet anyone else."

We all chuckled, and Sierra said, "Well, my future boyfriend is busy writing incredible songs that the whole world will sing along to one day!"

I kept wiping the counter, but I was smiling.

"How about you, Allie?" joked Sierra. "What's Colin up to right now?"

I swiped at her with the rag, and she jumped away, shrieking.

"I don't even know where Colin is these days!" I said, trying to keep my voice light.

"Wait. Haven't you texted him since you got back from camp?" asked Tamiko.

I shrugged.

"Why not?" asked Sierra. "The last time I saw him, he asked me when you'd be back."

"He did?" I tried to hide my smile.

Sierra nodded. "Maybe he doesn't know you're home."

"Allie, he's, like, your best friend at Vista Green. Why haven't you told him you're back?" said Tamiko. "That's weird."

"I . . . I just didn't want to seem like I was stalking him."

"You weirdo! How would it be stalking to tell a close friend that you're home after being away for a long time?"

I shrugged again.

"Were you hoping his love radar would make him magically sense you were back and he'd just appear?" Tamiko teased.

I swatted her with the rag, but she wasn't completely wrong. I had told Colin more or less when I'd be home, and I had hoped he'd be keeping track and contact me as soon as I'd returned. But he hadn't.

"Maybe *he's* worried about acting like a stalker," said Sierra thoughtfully. She was so kind that she always looked at every side of a situation.

I hadn't really thought of it that way, but I pushed that idea out of my mind. I still wanted *him* to come find *me*! "Maybe," I said.

Tamiko and Sierra exchanged a glance. "Don't be a shy little turtle," said Tamiko. "You have to stick your neck out sometimes."

Sierra pushed her head forward like a turtle to illustrate, and we all giggled.

It was all well and good for Sierra to stick her neck out, but I was a shy little turtle. I'd do anything to avoid sticking my neck out. Even if that meant not texting a so-called crush.

CHAPTER TWO

I LOVE FOOD—AND WRITING ABOUT IT TOO!

I checked my SuperSnap account one last time before I powered down my phone. Colin wasn't the best social media user even during the school year, but I'd hoped he would at least post a few photos so I could see where he was. Like, was he even *in* Bayville right now? And if so, where was he?

I sighed and then took a deep breath in for courage, like my dad had taught me. I was outside my new classroom at the Y and was ready to learn all about food writing for three hours a day, two mornings a week. What I *wasn't* ready for was a sea of new faces.

I gripped the doorknob and pushed with a sweaty palm. The door didn't open. I could see kids sitting inside and the teacher at the desk. It didn't look like they had started yet, but it was one minute before start time. I pushed again. Was the door locked? I gave the doorknob a rattle, and a bunch of people looked up at the door. My face started a slow burn from the bottom up; the feeling of the heat rising in my cheeks made me even more embarrassed, so I blushed harder. I'm sure my face was scarlet. I gave the door one more yank, and in doing so, I also somehow pulled it, and the door opened.

Pull, not push. Good one, Allie.

I stumbled into the classroom awkwardly, and a few of the kids giggled. Not meanly, but it was still embarrassing that they had noticed me at all.

"Good morning!" said the teacher cheerfully.

I mumbled a "good morning" and headed to the last row of the classroom. Just as I set my bag down on the desk, the teacher called, "We're not too big a group, so let's all try to stay toward the front of the room, please. It makes for better conversation, okay?"

Everyone swiveled to look at me. I nodded, trudged back toward the front of the room, and selected a seat behind a very large boy, who would hide me well.

Phew. Safe.

I settled into my seat and darted a few glances around at the other kids. From what I could see, there were around sixteen of us, equally split between boys and girls, some a little older than I was, but not super-old. Probably early high school, like ninth graders.

"All right. I think it's time we get started!" said the teacher, standing up at the front of the classroom. "I'm Valerie Gallo, and I'm super-excited to be your instructor for this course. I love cooking and food, and talking and writing about cooking and food, and I am really looking forward to getting to know you all. I think we'll cook up some great things in this course together, haha!"

Everyone chuckled politely, and Ms. Gallo grinned.

I recognized her name from her byline in our local paper, the *Daily Chronicle*. She was one of the two food writers on staff there, and she often reviewed local restaurants. Her food descriptions always made my mouth water. I was psyched that I was going to hear her instructions on food writing.

Ms. Gallo had us go around the room and introduce ourselves. Because I was in the back, I went last, and by the time they got to me, I was in a state of total panic at having to speak. The other kids had said their names, grades, and schools, and then had given some detail about their passions for food and/or writing. I just wanted to get it over with, so I didn't plan to go into much detail.

"I . . . uh . . . I'm Allie Shear. I'll be an eighth grader at Vista Green . . . and I love food!" I babbled nervously.

"Welcome, Allie!" said Ms. Gallo with a warm smile. "Well, let's get started! Is anyone here familiar with M. J. Connor's work?"

Of course! I thought excitedly. She was one of my favorite writers of all time. My school librarian, Mrs. K., had given me one of her books to read this year. M. J. Connor was one of the most acclaimed food writers ever, and she had basically invented food writing as a genre. I adored her work.

I was nodding at Ms. Gallo, but when I looked around and realized that no one else was, I quickly stilled my bobbing head. The last thing I wanted was for the teacher to notice and call on me to explain anything about Connor and her work in front of all these other kids. Luckily, the boy in front of me—Sam—had hidden my nodding head from her view.

"Okay. Well, then let me tell you about her and

her glorious food writing," said Ms. Gallo. "One of my favorite things about her work is her choice of words. Certainly, all writing comes down to word choice." She laughed a little. "But let's think about how in food writing, just the right word can make all the difference between good and bad. Think of 'crisp green lettuce' and 'limp green lettuce.' A big difference, right? Or look at peanut butter—chunky or smooth? It's all in the choice of words. . . . Try to keep from being too *ordinary*, as blandness is the kiss of death in writing *and* in cooking. . . ."

And we were off and running, and I was in heaven.

Ever since Molly's had been interviewed for articles in the local paper and for a gourmet food website, I'd been into food writing. I wrote a column for my school newspaper called Get the Scoop, where I reviewed books and then suggested an ice cream treat to pair with the book while the person was reading it. The column had been popular, and Colin had even told me once that his older sister (who was in high school) read it religiously. Crazy!

Between brainstorming flavors with my mom, watching Tamiko concoct wild parfaits and promotional ice cream sundaes, and reading food writing in magazines and books suggested by Mrs. K., I'd had a pretty foodie year. Plus, Tamiko and Sierra and I adored going to the food truck park at our local mall and trying new dishes all the time. I loved the fact that good food writing inspired so many of my senses—I could picture the food and imagine the smell and taste, as well as the texture in my mouth. The best food writing made me instantly hungry and excited, and it was a skill I'd love to develop. Maybe someday I could have a job like Ms. Gallo's, and combine food and writing for a living. That would be so ideal.

Now Ms. Gallo was up at the SMART Board, asking us for descriptive words that would be good for food writing. Kids were calling out as she scribbled in green marker.

"Crispy!"

"Juicy!"

"Thick!"

I had so many words that I could call out, but I was too shy.

"Let's hear from the back row," said Ms. Gallo, as if reading my mind.

I thought of M. J. Connor and one of my favorite

excerpts from her description of a meal in France. "Cushioned," I croaked in a voice rusty from disuse.

"Yes!" cried Ms. Gallo. "Who said that?"

Tentatively I raised my hand.

"Um, Allie?"

I nodded.

"Have you read M. J. Connor?"

I nodded again.

Ms. Gallo grinned. "Great. Are you thinking of 'Cushions of toast softened with creamy pats of sweet butter'?"

I grinned back and nodded yet again.

"Nice," said Ms. Gallo, a glint of admiration in her eye. "Who else?" she asked as she looked around the room.

This happened to me a lot: I always befriended the teacher. Somehow it was safer than dealing directly with the other kids, and it created a little bubble for me so that I didn't really need to interact with anyone else.

The morning went on with us collecting words and copying them down, and Ms. Gallo quoting her favorite writers and recommending books for us to read. It was kind of freewheeling, though she said that once we had each written a piece to work with, probably by the next class, we'd split up into more of a workshop setting, with kids in small groups or partnerships for half of each class. Ugh. *Awk*-ward! I was not looking forward to *that*.

"Your assignment!" Ms. Gallo announced as the clock struck noon. "Write a review of an exciting restaurant. Bonus points if you go and actually have a meal there between now and Thursday's class! I want five hundred words. No groans! You can do it. Remember to account for ambiance and service as well as the food. Thanks for coming today, and good luck! *Bon appétit!*"

I quickly packed my things and rushed out. I was due to work at Molly's at one o'clock, and the bus ride would take twenty minutes at least. That's what I told myself, anyway. It was more that I really didn't want to have to chat with anyone.

As I speed-walked out of the building and down the block to the bus stop, my heart raced with a feeling of exhilaration. I was thrilled by the teacher and the class, but I was even more thrilled that I'd escaped without having to interact with any of the kids. What a relief to not have to do the whole awkward getting-to-know-you conversation with any randoms (to use Tamiko's word). Maybe I could partner with the teacher for the workshop in the next class. It would be oh-so-much easier.

On the bus I powered up my phone and checked Colin's SuperSnap again. Nothing.

My fingers hovered over the screen as I debated whether or not to text him. I had his contact info right there in the palm of my hand, and I missed him. Would it be so awful if I sent a breezy little text? Maybe something like, "Hey, Colin. Hope your summer is great so far! Stop by for an ice cream at Molly's on the house so I can hear all about it!" But was the free ice cream part desperate? Like, was I bribing him to come see me? And if I didn't say "on the house," was I basically asking him to come and spend money to see me? But how else could I phrase it? Ugh.

Totally befuddled, I locked the phone, dropped it back into my bag, and stared out the window. I thought about asking Tamiko for advice, but then I realized she was on the plane, flying across the Pacific Ocean. I missed her already.

Monday afternoons at Molly's were pretty quiet, it turned out, even in the summer. Probably because so many people got ice cream on the weekends and Mondays were all business for them, but it made for a slow afternoon.

Sierra and I were both working, but there really wasn't enough for us to do. The topping jars and bins were all full, the counters and floor sparkling, the bathroom shining, and the ice cream freezer bursting with fresh bins of cool ice cream flavors. Even the few customers seemed a little uninspired on a Monday. One lady ordered a vanilla shake. A plain vanilla shake! Tamiko never would have stood for an order like that if she were there. She would have encouraged the woman to think outside the box and order something great, or convinced her to let Tamiko surprise her with a creation. But without Tamiko there, Sierra and I just smiled and made the shake and rang up the lady's order. Ho hum.

In between helping customers, Sierra sang some new songs she'd written, to test them out on me and get my reaction.

"I'm just a lonely girl. Are you lonely too? Maybe I'm the girl for you," Sierra sang out. "And then I'll point to the audience. What do you think?"

"It's okay," I said slowly.

"Just okay?" Sierra looked at me seriously. "Come on. You're holding back. I can tell. What don't you like about it?"

"No, no, no, I don't mean I don't like it," I said. "It's just . . . a little . . ." I searched for the right word, thinking of Ms. Gallo and her focus on word choice. "Ordinary?"

Sierra looked confused. "I don't understand."

I sighed. "'Lonely *too*. I'm the girl for *you*.' What's the next verse? 'Without you I'll go *boo-hoo*'?"

Thankfully, Sierra didn't get insulted; she just laughed.

"I'm sorry," I said. "It's just that some of the other songs you sing have such meaningful words. I know pop music is supposed to be light, but I just think you can do a little more with this one."

Sierra nodded in agreement. "Maybe it's because there's not a special person in my life to think about while I sing it," Sierra said. "You know, the way Tamiko has Ewan, and you"—Sierra paused for dramatic effect, and her eyes sparkled—"have Colllllllin." She sang his name out.

I blushed. "I don't 'have' Colin," I said. "He's just a friend. A friend I . . . maybe kinda sorta like. A little bit." Why did I always get flustered talking about Colin?

"Well, that's still more than I have," Sierra said. "All I have is my cat," she sang loudly to no one in particular. "Where are youuuuuu, my little pet? I'm missing you, and we haven't even met!" Sierra turned to me with a grin. "Hey, that's pretty good. I'm gonna write that down so I don't *forget*. Haha!"

The two customers who were sitting at a table clapped. Sierra took a silly bow. "I'll be signing autographs before you leave!" she joked, and they smiled and nodded. "See?" she said to me. "I knew it was good!"

I rolled my eyes, but I had to smile, too. *Even when she's just fooling around, Sierra finds a way to connect with people,* I marveled. I could barely even speak in a room full of people who shared my interests, never mind break out into song in front of total strangers.

I thought of school this past year and how long it had taken me to speak up, even with great encouragement from, say, my favorite teacher—Ms. Healy. She'd worked so hard to get me to talk in English class, enticing me with little tidbits that she knew about me from conversations we'd had outside of class; bringing up my favorite book, *Anne of Green Gables*; asking me point-blank questions I couldn't squirm away from. It had finally worked. By the end of the year I'd been able to speak out loud in her class every day.

I also thought about the school librarian, Mrs. K., and how she'd drawn me out with all of her little kindnesses—taking me to the Book Fest at my old school and giving me great things to read. (Hello, M. J. Connor!)

Colin, too, had made an effort with me, inviting me to sit with him on the school bus, saving me from the girls we called the Mean Team, and asking me to write for the school paper. We were actual friends. He was the first friend I'd really made on my own, since my mom had basically picked Sierra and Tamiko for me when we were toddlers—so Colin being the first friend I had chosen myself was kind of significant.

I didn't have a ton of other friends at school, and I generally kept to myself. If I disappeared from Vista Green, I wasn't sure too many people would notice, beyond Colin and those two teachers. Maybe also

Amanda, whose mom lived in my dad's building. We were friends, you could say. I probably would have been hanging with her if she hadn't been at camp for the summer. But I was always relieved to get home at the end of the school day and be alone—to nestle into my window seat at my mom's or into my comfy marshmallow armchair at my dad's. The way I'd felt like I'd escaped from food-writing class, that was kind of how I felt every day when I got home from school.

But now that I'd been away from school for five weeks or so, it all felt like a dream. Had I really switched schools this last year? Left my two besties and everything I knew behind? Had I really worked in the library and written for the school paper? Had I really tutored kids at the town library? I guessed I had, but it was hard to imagine doing it all again. I dreaded restarting it all, rekindling the relationships, just as I dreaded having to interact with all new kids in my food-writing class. It would be so much easier to just hide at home with a book!

The two customers stood up to leave, and Sierra looked up from the notebook where she was writing down lyrics. "Good-bye, my darling fans!" she called after them. "I'll be performing every weekday afternoon, from one to six, and Sundays from one to eight. Come on back!"

They laughed and waved and promised to return, while I shook my head in amazement.

"Oh, Sierra, you are too much!"

"In a good way or a bad way?" she asked with a smile, but her eyes were serious.

"In just the right way," I said. *For you,* I added silently. *Not the right way for me at all!*

CHAPTER THREE

MAKING NEW FRIENDS IS HARD

When we left work on Monday evening, I invited Sierra to go to dinner with me the next night at a new vegetarian food truck, Dirt Treats, at the mall. I needed a place to review for class and figured something brand-new would be ideal. Plus, I was dying to try their Amazing UnBurger—a vegetarian meat alternative that supposedly looked, smelled, and tasted like regular meat. Most likely no one else in my class would have tried it yet, and my take on it would be fresh.

So on Tuesday at six fifteen, Sierra and I were in my dad's car headed to the food-truck park, and my dad was asking Sierra all about her summer.

"Oh, Mr. Shear, rock-band camp was so awesome.

I met so many kids, it was incredible. They're so talented and inspiring, and we've all stayed in touch, and we share info and try out new material on one another almost every day. We're always sending snaps with little clips of us performing, and then we give one another advice. It's been amazing. I have so many new friends from it!"

"Sierra, that's wonderful!" said my dad. "That is probably the best you could ever hope for from a camp. I know Allie loves her camp friends as well, but they don't really stay in touch as much during the year."

I bristled. "We do too. We snap . . . sometimes. And we, like, send one another texts . . . now and then. It's just . . . a lot of work to keep up with people you don't see a lot."

Sierra smiled at me kindly. "I know. If my campmates weren't local or into the same stuff as I am, I probably wouldn't be talking to them all the time either."

Right.

She continued, "Plus, they're nothing like the deep relationships you have with your camp friends after all these years, Allie. I mean, my new friends are fun, but they're new. We don't have years of history like you do." She smiled again.

I felt a little better. "Exactly."

My dad's eyes met mine in the rearview mirror, and he smiled encouragingly. "Old friends are the best friends."

"Yes," I agreed. I had a funny feeling that they were both trying to make me feel better about something, but I couldn't put my finger on what it was.

Sierra and I hopped out of the car near the entrance to the food-truck park, and my dad gave me twenty dollars and told us to have a good time. I had my notebook and a pen to take notes with—I found it smoother to handwrite when I was researching something, rather than typing notes onto my tiny phone screen—and I was determined to get things just right for my first assignment.

It was a warm and clear night with a breeze, and the place was buzzing. All the fairy lights along the fence were twinkling, and the cooking smells of all the delicious foods mingled into one yummy feast for my nose. I sniffed deeply and happily and picked up my pace. Suddenly I was starving.

"Okay, it should be right along here on this side," I said to Sierra.

"I'm game! I love trying new foods. Ooh, there are a lot of people here tonight, aren't there? For a Tuesday?"

She was right. As we arrived at the Dirt Treats truck, we realized there was a long line.

"Bummer!" I said. There were probably twenty or thirty people in front of us.

"I guess we all had the same idea!" said Sierra. "Oh, look! There's my friend Dylan from rock-band camp!" She waved at him, and he waved back, gesturing that he'd come say hi after he got his order in. Sierra nodded enthusiastically and continued to look all around to see if there was anyone else she recognized. That was when I realized there was someone I recognized. Actually, more than someone. There were three people in line—not together, all separate—from my food-writing class at the Y! And one of them was right in front of us—the big guy, Sam, who'd sat right in front of me the day before. My human shield.

I raised my eyebrows at Sierra and indicated with a jerk of my head that I knew the kid.

She raised her eyebrows back and tipped her

head at him in confirmation. I nodded and mouthed, "Food-writing class." And before I could say anything else, Sierra was tapping him on the shoulder.

Noooooo!

Sam turned around and looked at Sierra quizzically.

"Hi! I'm Sierra. This is my friend Allie. Do you recognize her?"

Sam turned to me and looked blank. Then a small look of recognition dawned on his face. "Food writing?" he asked pleasantly.

I nodded as my face burned in embarrassment. I wanted to stare daggers at Sierra, but I couldn't with him looking at me. "Hi," I said awkwardly.

"What's your name again?" he asked.

"Allie," I croaked nervously. I hoped he'd turn back around and that would be that. I also hoped the line would suddenly pick up steam and he'd have to focus on moving up. But we were all stuck in this holding pattern.

"I'm Sam. Nice to see you here. Have you tried this truck before?" He was totally comfortable making conversation.

I shook my head and glanced at Sierra, who was gesturing at me to say more.

"Uh, no . . . I've been dying to try the Amazing UnBurger, though," I answered.

"Me too!" said Sam with a big smile. "There's just no way it's as good as people say! I'm a total meat-and-potatoes guy, and my soft spot is barbecue, so I am really dying to try this thing. I'm gonna write about it for our assignment. Are you?"

"Yeah. I was thinking I would."

"Cool. I bet those kids are too." He gestured to the other two kids I'd recognized from class. "Let's all sit together. If you hold my spot, I'll go ask them, okay?"

"Oh. What? Yeah. Um . . ."

He hesitated, his eyebrows knit together. "Is that all right? I mean, are you two looking for company?"

"NO! I mean, yes, let's sit together. Okay. Thanks. Good. Right. I'll hold your spot."

His face relaxed into an easy smile. "Great. I'll go tell them. Maybe one of them can snag us a table after they order."

"Okay," I said tentatively.

After he stepped away, Sierra smiled. "He seems nice."

"Why did you do that?" I exploded. "Now I have

to meet all these people and, like, make small talk all night!"

Sierra looked surprised. "What? You didn't want to talk to him? But he's in your class!"

"That doesn't mean I need to talk to him!" I protested.

"Do you mean to tell me you would have stood here on line behind him and never said a word?"

I folded my arms across my chest. "Yes!"

Sierra was incredulous. "But why? You know him. You have stuff in common. You're going to be seeing him for, like, six hours a week for three weeks. Why wouldn't you want to be friends?"

"Just . . . I don't know. It's so much work!"

"Work?" Sierra laughed. "You think it's work to talk to people?"

I nodded.

"Even me?" she asked.

"Not really you, or Tamiko. I mean, once I know people, it's not as much work."

"But how are you going to get to know more people if you don't talk to them?"

"Why do I need to know more people? I have you guys."

Sierra laughed in surprise. "But don't you want more friends?"

"Why?"

"I don't know. To learn from? To have fun? What if Tamiko and I were both away? Who would you come here with?"

I looked away so she wouldn't see the tears that had suddenly sprung into my eyes. I clenched my jaw and willed the tears back into my tear ducts.

"Allie?" Sierra asked quietly.

I turned back to her. "What?"

"Do you *like* having friends?"

"Of—of course!" I sputtered. "I like *having* them. I just don't like *making* them."

Sierra frowned, deep in thought. "It's hard to *have* them if you don't *make* them first! But seriously, for me . . . I think *making* friends is easier than having them. New friends don't expect anything from you. You can keep things easy-breezy. Older friends need reliability, checking in, maintenance—"

"Thanks a lot!" I said, but her comment made me smile.

"You know what I mean. I'm not as good at

all the obligations that go along with maintaining friendships, but I can chat with almost anyone."

She was right, actually.

"Have you ever read about the sixteen personality types?" she asked.

I shook my head as I watched Sam chat easily with one of our classmates. He was just like Sierra—meeting new people was no problem for him.

"It's really cool. We learned about it in English this year. There's this famous psychiatrist who said that everyone in the world—or in fiction, which is why we were studying it—can be sorted into one of sixteen 'archetypes,' or basic personalities. You can go online and take a personality test and find out which one you are. It's pretty cool how accurate it is. Anyway, I think our big difference is that I'm an extrovert and you're an introvert."

"What does that mean?" I asked as Sam made his way back to us.

"In short, I get energy from social interaction, and you get it from being alone."

"Oh, great! I'm destined for a life of loneliness!" I said.

"Don't be silly. It's not like that. Just look it up

online when you get home. 'Sixteen personalities.'"

"Okeydokey," I agreed.

Sam had returned. "They're in. Taylor's going to grab us all a table, and then we can sit together and compare notes . . . and word choices!" he joked.

I smiled. "Great," I said, crossing my fingers at the white lie.

"Super-fun!" said Sierra, and I knew she actually meant it.

"Juicy."

"Thick."

"Salty."

"Crunchy."

"Crisp."

"Gooey."

"Gross! Gooey?" said Anika. We all laughed.

"Well, the special sauce and cheese on mine were gooey," explained Sam as he looked at his notes. We were all comparing word choices to describe the burgers we'd just eaten, which had turned out to be delicious, even after the long wait.

Despite my misgivings, I was having a great time. Taylor, Anika, and Sam from my class were all super easygoing and friendly, and their warmth carried me along. They all just assumed I was friendly too, and with Sierra there to grease the wheels of social interaction, everything was running smoothly. Plus, the three of them were as into food and writing as I was, and it was really cool to be hanging with kids who were interested in the same stuff. I guessed that was how Sierra felt about rock-band camp and Tamiko felt about her photo class.

It was just about time for us to head out. I'd told my dad to expect to pick us up around eight, and it was already eight thirty. I'd texted him five minutes earlier, and we needed to be out at the gate so he didn't have to circle.

"Hey, you guys. Sierra and I have to go. My dad will be here any minute. Sam, thanks for organizing us all. I'll see everyone in class on Thursday."

Just as we were standing up to go, who should walk up but . . . Colin!

"Colin!" I said in shock.

"Allie!" He grinned. "When did you get back?" He looked around the table at the other kids and, recognizing no one, looked back at me in surprise.

"Um, five days ago." Had it been that long already?

Longer, maybe? Eek. It'd been more than ten days now.

"*Five* days?" he echoed incredulously as his smile faded. I could feel everyone at the table watching us. "Wow," he said, shaking his head as if to clear it. "Okay. Wow. Well . . . see you around." And he turned and walked away.

I stood there in shock, my mouth actually hanging open, until Sierra put her hand on my elbow. "Hey, Alley Cat, let's go meet your dad. Bye, everyone!" she said cheerfully.

But they were all looking at me like they'd just seen something they shouldn't have.

"Bye, you guys. See you, Allie," Sam and Anika said quietly.

I walked away from the table like a zombie, still watching Colin's back as he crossed the open square. I felt horrible.

I ditched my stuff in the trash and stowed the tray on top. As we walked out to the parking lot, I stammered, "Um—that was bad—I think."

Sierra bit her lip. "We *told* you to text him."

I spun around angrily, taking out my embarrassment on her. "And I told *you*: I didn't want him to think I like him!"

"But you *do* like him! And besides, he's your friend! That's not how you treat friends!"

"What would you know about it anyway? You just admitted that you're bad at keeping friends." Oh. Had I really just said that out loud?

"Is that what you actually think?" Sierra's eyes were bright with angry tears as my dad pulled up.

"I don't know what I think. Let's just go!"

We climbed into the car and didn't speak again for the whole ride home.

CHAPTER FOUR

KEEPING OLD FRIENDS IS HARD TOO

Within a half hour of arriving home at my dad's, I texted an apology to Sierra.

I'm sorry, Sierra. Did not mean to take it out on you. I'm just upset about Colin. You are much better than me with friends. Look how many you have.

I deleted the last line because it made me seem like I was competing with her. Then I pressed send and waited to see if she'd reply.

While I waited, I took out my computer and searched for the sixteen personalities thing that Sierra had mentioned, then settled in to take a test that would tell me what my type was. The questions were things like, was I a planner or did I just wing things? (Uh, planner! Duh!) Was I outgoing or shy in social settings? (No-brainer.) Some of the questions were more for adults, like about relationships or whatever, so I just substituted how I was with Colin or my friends, and then sat back to wait for what felt like a diagnosis from the website.

The result was: I was a Logistician. That meant I was responsible, honest, reliable, and analytical, and that I liked rules, regulations, and systems. Hmm. A lot of the traits were incredibly accurate, but some were a bummer and it made me feel grumpy. I was steady and reliable but also, reading between the lines, kind of boring and unimaginative.

I snapped shut the computer, and my phone buzzed with an incoming text.

Thx, Sierra had written.

Hmm. She was still mad, I could tell. I wrote a new text:

Thank you for organizing a fun, spontaneous night with my classmates. See you tomorrow. Xo

I pressed send and set down my phone, not expecting a reply.

But the phone buzzed a second later.

Text Colin!

Grrr. Now I was *really* grumpy. I stared at the

phone and tried to imagine what I'd say to him.

"Hey, Colin. I'm sorry I didn't let you know I was home. I've been so busy! How is your summer going?"

My thumbs hovered over the screen without typing. Anything I said would seem lame at this point. I realized now that I was bad at making new friends, *and* bad at keeping old ones. I threw down my phone in disgust, brushed my teeth, and got ready for bed, all the while thinking of my personality type and how it said I was "slow to make friends" and tended to have a "small inner circle." Even though this was true, it irritated me. I didn't like thinking of myself as a predictable type, and I was annoyed that the diagnosis had been so spot-on.

I called good night to my dad, flipped off the overhead light, and got under the covers. He came in to say good night and talk about plans for the next day. Even though I was too old to be "tucked into bed," I still liked that my dad came in to say good night, since I didn't get to see him every day now that he and my mom had divorced.

"Is everything okay with you and Sierra?" he asked. "You two were awfully quiet on the way home."

I sighed. "Yeah. I think we're good now."

He ruffled my hair, guaranteeing bed head for me the next day. "Okay. Let me know if you ever need to talk anything through. You two are such old friends, and I know there can be ups and downs. When I was your age, George and I didn't speak for a whole year. Can you imagine?" He clicked off the bedside light.

George was my godfather and my dad's best and oldest friend. I *couldn't* imagine them going that long without speaking.

"Why?" I asked, swallowing nervously. With only three real friends, I couldn't spare losing one for a year!

"Something about a girl. We were immature and stubborn. It was a waste of time. My advice to you is this: don't let things fester between you and your friends. Nip problems in the bud. Be direct. And let me know anytime you'd like to talk. Good night, sweetheart. Love you."

"Love you, Dad."

In the dim light from the streetlamp outside, I stared at the ceiling. I'd started out talking about Sierra, but my friendship with Colin was in danger too. I rolled onto my side. I hadn't nipped *that* problem in the bud, and now it might be too late. I thought about asking Tamiko for advice—she gave great advice—but I didn't want to bug her on her vacation, especially for boy advice, friendship or otherwise. Tamiko was great at sharing wisdom about romance, but it kind of annoyed her to do it.

I decided I would handle this on my own.

At work the next day Sierra was normal, thank goodness, and I quickly relaxed into our usual comfortable companionship. The store was empty and I was mopping the floor, when suddenly Sierra squealed.

"Oooh! We got a snap from Tamiko!"

"No way!" I did a last swab of the floor and put the mop aside for a moment. Then I pulled out my phone to see.

Tamiko had sent a photo of herself hugging her grandfather, and she was wearing a cute new minidress in vivid shades of purple and red. In her hand she held some kind of fried food that peeked out of a small paper bag.

Kon'nichiwa, besties! she'd written. I'm having a great visit with my grandfather. He's so happy to see all of us. Today I went shopping in Harajuku in the city and found lots of cool stuff, like this dress

I'm wearing. Who would have ever thought of wearing purple and red together? But somehow it works, right? Also, I tried the best sweet treat ever—a long, crunchy cream puff. YUM! Maybe we can do them at Molly's! Miss you guys! Xoxo

My heart pinched at the sight of my beloved bestie, now so far away. I missed her terribly and needed her. Swallowing the lump in my throat, I shook my head in amazement. "Tamiko can make any outfit look good," I said, in a lighter tone than I felt.

Sierra agreed. "Just watch. Tamiko will wear that dress to school once, and suddenly red-and-purple combos will be the next big thing."

"Where's Harajuku?" I asked.

"Hmm." Sierra's fingers flew across the screen of her phone. "Harajuku," she typed. Zillions of hits came up as I watched over her shoulder.

"Let's check this out," Sierra said, clicking on a YouTube video called "Tour of Harajuku!"

While we watched a series of brief videos, Sierra's phone kept buzzing with new notifications. People were snapping her, commenting on her snaps, texting her, e-mailing, the works. Sierra declined each notification automatically, without even reading it. It was like she got so many that she couldn't even be bothered, whereas if I got a notification—they were few and far between—I would be so excited that I would immediately click to open it.

Instinctively I glanced at my own phone—nothing from *anyone.*

We were still studying the videos—it turned out that Harajuku was a trendy shopping neighborhood—when we heard someone cough. We both looked up and realized there was a line of eight people waiting for ice cream!

"Oh my gosh, I'm so sorry!" I gasped. Sierra and I sprang into action, scooping and swirling, ringing people up, and just flying through orders.

Most of the people were fine once we got going, but I could see that one or two were still annoyed. Trying to make up for the wait, I gave each order a generous helping of sprinkles instead of the tiny "sprinkle of happy" I usually added.

"An extra sprinkle of happy," I told the customers. "Thank you for your patience while we did our flavor research!"

Luckily, it worked, and they all walked away with a smile. When everyone had been served, I allowed myself a deep breath, and Sierra and I looked at each other in relief.

"Thank goodness my mom didn't bust us on the phone! She might have fired us both," I whispered, so that the customers seated at the tables couldn't hear our conversation.

"I know! Bad employees!" said Sierra, but she giggled, and then I giggled, and soon we both were laughing in relief.

Sierra looked out the big plate-glass window at the front of the store, where some abandoned clutter and trash were visible. "I'm going to go wipe the outdoor tables and check the garbage bin out there."

I nodded. There was lots to wipe up inside after that brief frenzy. I rinsed out the cleaning cloth and set about making everything neat and tidy again. But a few minutes later, when I happened to look out the window, I gasped. Colin was outside, and he was talking to Sierra! I darted a quick glance at my reflection in the mirror along one side of the store. My hair was mussed. I tucked it back into place, retied my apron neatly, and didn't try to hide the smile that had bloomed on my face. Colin had come! I hadn't even had to text him! We were such good friends that he'd just automatically forgiven me and shown up. Yay!

I watched their conversation taking place. They were both chatting and smiling. I could see them wrapping it up, and my smile bloomed even larger as I got ready for Colin to enter the store. But then . . . he didn't. He and Sierra fist-bumped, and he walked away. He hadn't even glanced inside.

What just happened?

The smile dropped from my face as Sierra entered instead. She still had a happy look on her face.

"Is he going to get money or something?" I asked anxiously. "I would have given him a free ice cream. I hope he knows that by now."

Sierra's smile now faded as quickly as mine had. In fact, she looked alarmed. "Um, I . . ."

"Is he not coming in here at all?" I spat as my nerves turned to anger.

"I don't know. He didn't say. I mean . . . I didn't get the impression he was even thinking of coming in. He . . . must've been on his way somewhere else?"

My blood was boiling now. "Did he say where?"

Sierra shook her head, her eyes wide.

"Did he ask about me?" I demanded quietly.

Again, Sierra shook her head, biting her lip now.

"Did you mention me?"

She just stared.

I put my hands on my hips. "Sierra!" I huffed.

I looked off to the side while we both stood there. It wasn't her fault. It was mine, I knew. I should have texted him the night before, or at least gone outside just now and said hi! It wouldn't have even mattered what I said. I put my head in my hands and slowly shook it from side to side.

Sierra came behind the counter and patted me gently on the back. "Don't worry, Allie. He seemed like he was in a rush. I'm sure . . . well . . ."

"It's okay, Sierra. It's all my fault. I know I've been a bad friend to him . . ."

I could hear Sierra's phone buzzing away in her pocket, all of her friends checking in, asking for feedback on songs, and making weekend plans. And I officially had one friend in this town now, and I hadn't been super-nice to her in the past twenty-four hours.

I looked at her. "Thanks for being such a good friend—"

Just then the door opened and a voice interrupted our private chat.

"Hey, rock star! Why don't you sing a song to

keep the customers entertained?" somebody said.

We turned to see Reagan, the drummer from Sierra's band, the Wildflowers. I liked Reagan, but I was annoyed by the interruption. I said a cool "Hi" and crouched down to pull supplies from the storage cabinets under the rear counter.

Sierra laughed. "I *should* sing a song! Anything to keep our customers happy!"

Reagan stepped up to the counter, ordered her usual (a Rockin' Rocky Road cone), and said to Sierra, "You know, I really liked that song idea you texted me about. I was trying to think of a name for it. How does 'Dear Future Crush' sound?"

"Oh my goodness, I love it!" Sierra exclaimed from her scooping position. She stood up and presented the cone to Reagan. "I think it will be really fun to write—and to sing, of course!"

"It's a great idea," Reagan said. "So relatable. I bet everyone looking for that special someone will be singing it!"

"I just can't seem to get the words right," said Sierra, turning with a smile to include me in the conversation as I sorted paper straws into a dispenser.

While they'd been chatting, a few people had

trickled into the shop and milled around, studying the menu board. But suddenly the customers were all ready to order at once. In fact, a small line had formed.

A man snorted. "So are you gonna sing, or take my order?"

I felt a little panicked. I set the straws aside and whisper-yelled, enjoying my moment of power. "Sierra, can you and Reagan finish your conversation later . . . like, when you're not at work?"

Sierra was immediately embarrassed and flustered. "Of course," she agreed speedily. "Call me later," she said to Reagan, who waved and left. Then Sierra turned back to the customer. "I'm so sorry for making you wait, sir," she said with a huge grin. "What super-delicious, yummy ice cream treat can I get you to cheer you up?"

The grumpy man suddenly smiled. "That's okay," he said, immediately charmed by Sierra's good nature and friendliness.

A lady also waiting in line spoke up. "Why don't you sing us your song while you make our sundaes, honey?"

Sierra laughed. "It's not written yet," she said. "It's

just an idea. But come back in ten days, and I promise I'll sing it for you!"

Everyone in the line laughed and clapped.

Once again I was amazed. *Sierra can charm anybody, anytime*, I thought. A little pang of jealousy thrummed in my chest, and it didn't feel good. First my missing Tamiko, then seeing all those texts and snaps on Sierra's phone, then being ignored by Colin, now watching Sierra get all the love. It reminded me of that book-turned-movie *Alexander and the Terrible, Horrible, No Good, Very Bad Day.*

I thought, *I think I'll move to Australia.*

With Tamiko far away and Colin out of the picture, I'd have only one less friend there than I had here.

CHAPTER FIVE

POETRY AND VEGGIE BURGERS

That night I sat at the computer at my mom's, my spiral notebook open at my side as I worked on my first piece for the food-writing class. I'd written down lots of impressions from that evening out—about the food, the weather, the crowds, the atmosphere and energy—and I was braiding it all together into one thick and juicy piece. I was really enjoying myself. Writing was definitely my happy place (along with reading). The whole world just melted away while I was doing it, and I felt a tingle of happiness all up and down my shoulders and arms as I typed.

The Amazing UnBurger had tasted so much like a grilled beef burger, I couldn't get over it. It was crispy on the outside with a salty crust, but the inside was tender and crumbly and reddish, and it had that meaty taste known as "umami"—the salty, savory flavor that makes your mouth water when you smell meat cooking. I couldn't believe the burger had been made with vegetables. Like, I actually could not wrap my mind around it.

The other girl from my class who'd been there that night, Anika, was a vegetarian, and the burger had been so realistically meatlike that she'd grown suspicious eating it. She'd kept asking the people who worked there if they were positive it was made with vegetables.

The Amazing UnBurger had been served on a pillowy, sweetish brioche bun that had been toasted on the inside so that it was crunchy, while the outside remained soft and easy to bite into. I'd had mine with just cheddar cheese and mustard, but the other kids had tried theirs with special sauce, lettuce, tomatoes, pickles, sautéed onions, and more.

The other things I'd tried at Dirt Treats were the zucchini fries (matchstick-cut pieces of zucchini rolled in flour, lightly fried until crisp, and then squirted with lemon juice and dusted with flaky sea salt), radishes with cold butter (sounds gross, but they were sour-tasty with a good snap to them), and gazpacho shooters (little tiny Dixie cups of chilled puréed tomato soup with crunchy minced veggies in it and tiny cubed croutons on top). They were all delish!

Besides the food, one of the things I liked about Dirt Treats was that they were very environmentally conscious. They had paper straws, limited napkins, bamboo utensils, and paper goods rather than any plastic. Also, their pulpy cardboard plates had tiny flower seeds embedded in them, so if the plates became litter, they would quickly disintegrate, and the flower seeds would have a chance to grow. Dirt Treats planted a tree locally for every pack of napkins they went through, and instead of a tip jar, the money jar on their counter was a collection for the Nature Conservancy. The place had a real identity and made delicious food, plus they were doing good in the world.

I wrote up my whole review, including the balmy night, the twinkly fairy lights, and the kids clustered around rough-planked picnic tables, and I gave Dirt Treats five stars. Then I did a word count on the piece, and it was only three hundred and fifty words. Ms. Gallo had wanted five hundred.

Oh no!

I slumped back in my seat. How on earth was I going to come up with a hundred and fifty more words about vegetables? I flipped through my notebook and tried to think of areas I could expand on. As I flipped, I thought absentmindedly about Sierra and how she had made that night so fun, and how if Tamiko had been there with us, it would have been even more fun, but in a different way.

Inspired, I lifted my pen, turned to a blank page, and began to jot down some notes on how different my two besties were.

One is the sun—burning fiercely,
Pulling all to her side.
One is the moon—always moving,
Riding a new tide.
One is fiery, gold, electric, and wild.
The other is cool, silver, [something], and styled.

I chewed on the top of my pen. I was stumped on the last line. What *was* Tamiko like? Opinionated, stylish, inventive. But still kind of private. Sierra was totally out there, giving everyone her all, holding nothing back. I wondered where Tamiko would fall on the sixteen personalities test. Sierra was for sure an extrovert—she needed to be interacting with people (preferably new people) to get energized. She craved new experiences and was always signing up for activities, biting off more than she could chew, just because something "sounded fun." Tamiko, despite her public blog and her sassy confidence, was an introvert like me, I thought. She liked working on her creative projects alone. She marched to the beat of her own drum, following exactly no one else. And she was pretty picky about friends, even though she was confident enough to talk to anyone, anywhere, anytime.

What if I'd had to put myself in this poem? What was I, right in the middle of the sun and the moon? Solid, reliable, never waxing or waning, setting or rising, just down to . . . earth! I was the earth!

But what rhymed with "earth," besides "dearth"? (I'd had to look that up.) Hmm. "Birth" and "mirth." A little forced. I sighed and set aside the notebook and pen, then stretched and stood up from my desk. What was I going to do about this food-writing piece? I stared down at my computer in annoyance, willing a hundred and fifty more words to appear on the document all by themselves, but no luck.

As my writing happiness trickled away, all of my annoyances came back. What was I going to do about Colin? Why did Sierra have such an easy time charming people? Why was Molly's turning into a music-themed rocker hangout? Why did Tamiko have to go away for so long, and right when I needed her most?

To procrastinate, I went back onto the sixteen personalities site. I wanted to see if I could dig out some good qualities associated with my type, or maybe some strategies to handle all my shortcomings. I had just gotten going when I was interrupted.

"Allie! Dinner!" called my mom.

I stomped out of my room and down the creaky stairs to the kitchen. My mom's new house was vintage and beachy, unlike my dad's all-new, renovated warehouse loft-style apartment with a pool on the top of the building. I liked both and felt lucky that I got to enjoy the two different lifestyles, but my mom's house was better for stomping. At my dad's there were neighbors underneath, so we had to be considerate.

In the kitchen Tanner was already at the table, his grubby hands and stained T-shirt just totally unappetizing. I slid into my chair with a huff.

"Mom, does this kid ever bathe?" I asked. "He's filthy!" I knew I was being snotty, but I felt real pleasure in being mean to him just then.

He looked at me innocently, then examined his hands and arms. He looked back at me again, confused, as if he didn't even see the streaks of dirt and the dark crust under his fingernails. "What?" he said, blinking.

I rolled my eyes.

My mom came to the table with a platter of Chicken Milanese—thin, salty cutlets, breaded and then fried until crispy, served with lemon slices for squeezing on top—and a bowl of fresh dressed salad. "Tanner, please go wash your hands before you eat. And I want you to take a long bath after dinner."

Tanner groaned, but he stood up and went to the sink to wash his hands. "I'll take a bath, but only if I can watch a movie while I do it."

My mom had started bribing him to bathe. She would set up her laptop on the closed lid of the toilet, and he could download a show or movie to watch while he was in the tub. Talk about spoiled!

"Most humans enjoy being clean," I said as I lifted a piece of chicken and then a scoop of salad onto my plate. I wouldn't let his grossness ruin my meal, though. Chicken Milanese was one of my favorite dinners, and my mom made it really well. I loved the combo of the crisp, hot chicken and the cold, bitter salad, all in one bite.

"So tell me about the writing class, sweetheart," Mom said. "I feel like I've been so busy that we haven't even had a chance to discuss it yet."

I filled my mom in on the teacher, the class, the assignment, Sierra's and my night out, and how things had gone with the other kids from the class.

"It was really good that Sierra was there, because she got us all connected," I said reluctantly.

"She's such an outgoing and gregarious kid. It's a wonderful quality," said my mom, slicing her chicken.

"Can I be done?" asked Tanner.

He'd eaten six pieces of chicken and exactly no salad.

My mom looked at him and then at the salad, and I could see her deciding whether or not to fight him about vegetables. She wavered and then gave in. "Fine, but take two carrot sticks from the fridge and eat them both. And don't let me find them in the trash under your desk like last week!"

"Okay, Veggie Police," said Tanner. Then he slid his plate into the dishwasher and exited.

I looked at my mom. "Are you going to just let him be fresh to you like that?"

My mom was stifling a smile. "Oh, Allie. Why are you so grumpy tonight?"

It bugged me that she found his antics funny. I thought he was just plain rude, and I knew that when I was his age, I'd never have gotten away with what he got away with.

"I'm not grumpy," I said, looking down and stabbing my salad repeatedly.

My mom wasn't eating. She sat and watched me struggle with my salad, which made me even more annoyed. "What's wrong, sweetheart?" she asked kindly.

Her kind tone penetrated my grumpy shield, and I crumbled into tears. "I'm an introvert!" I wailed.

"What?" my mom was perplexed. I'd started in the middle.

Through my tears I explained about the sixteen personalities, and Sierra's charm, and my shyness with Colin and, well, everyone else in the world, and how I was doomed to be alone because I was a Logistician, and I wished I were an extrovert. And why hadn't she forced me to have more playdates when I was little?

My mom stood and grabbed some tissues off the counter, then sat next to me, wrapping her arm warmly and firmly around my shoulders. I bent into her neck and sobbed for a little bit while she patted my shoulder and doled out tissues.

Finally my sobs died out and I lifted my head and blotted my eyes. I blew my nose and cleared my throat.

"Better?" asked my mom with a small smile.

I shook my head.

Her smile turned into a frown as she studied me. "What's all this about introverts and extroverts and logistics?" she asked.

I sighed and explained about the archetypes and the test and my personality diagnosis.

My mom was aghast. "Allie! Don't be silly. There are billions and billions of people in the world. Do you really think they can all be broken down into one of sixteen types? Not to mention, you're twelve years old! You still have years to grow and change and follow your interests. Don't get upset over one website."

I was dumbfounded. "Wait, what?"

"Look, it's just like a quiz in a magazine. They ask you general questions, you give general answers, and they put you in a general category. That's all it is. You could take the test on a different day, be in a different mood when you answer the questions, and get assigned to a totally different category." She shook her head in disbelief.

"But I *am* an introvert!"

She shrugged. "Maybe so. But I was an introvert when I was your age, and now I'm an extrovert. Either category is fine, by the way. Plus, people can change, you know. And anyway, haven't you ever heard of an ambivert?"

I giggled at the funny word.

She nodded. "Yes! It's a thing! Some people are intro- and extroverts! There's a whole book about it that came out a few years ago. You should read *that*."

"Huh," I said in surprise. A weight was lifting from my shoulders a little. "So I'm not doomed to a small circle of friends for life just because I'm slow to make new friends?"

"Oh, Allie! How awful. Of course not! You can do or be whatever you want!"

"Then what I want is to be more like Sierra," I said. I explained how everything came so easily to Sierra, and how whenever she messed up or met new people or anything nerve-racking, she was just able to charm everyone by singing or being funny or nice or whatever.

"It is good to have an employee who knows how to keep our customers happy," my mom said. "I understand what you're feeling. However, you also need to remember that you're only seeing one aspect of Sierra's life. I'm sure there are other situations where she feels uncomfortable and unsure. No one is perfect at everything all the time."

I thought of how Sierra often overextended herself, saying yes to too many people, too many activities and plans. I sighed.

"Instead of being envious of Sierra for the way she is, maybe think of changes you'd like to make yourself," continued my mom.

"Don't expect me to start singing," I grumped. "I can't carry a tune. I'm tone-deaf. I'd scare the customers away!"

My mom laughed. "Too bad. I was just getting ready to promote Molly's as the only ice cream parlor with an all-singing staff. Kidding! No, what I meant was, think of things that make you feel good about yourself, instead of focusing on things about Sierra that make you envious."

"I guess," I agreed. "I hate feeling jealous of one of my best friends. And I'm annoyed that she's turning Molly's into a rocker hangout."

My mom smiled. "She has brought in some nice business with all those musical friends of hers. But why don't you add in some nice Allie touches? What ever happened to your book and ice cream pairings? You did those for the school paper, so why not do some right in the shop? People loved those!"

I nodded, trying to think of more Allie touches I could add to the store. I wished Tamiko were there to brainstorm with me. She always had outlandish ideas, and we were very creative together. Missing her made my heart ache and gave me an idea.

"Mom, is there any chance I could FaceTime with Tamiko sometime?"

My mom tipped her head to the side while she considered it. "I don't see why not. You'll just need to set up the call in advance so you're both in position at the same time."

I stood, excited, and cleared my plate, then put it in the dishwasher. I couldn't wait to get upstairs and contact Tamiko to set up our video chat. Maybe she could finally make me feel better. I hated feeling this way about one of my best friends.

CHAPTER SIX

TAMIKO TO THE RESCUE

With my Tamiko call scheduled for eight thirty the next morning, I was up as early as a bird. I showered and got dressed, had breakfast, packed my bag for writing class and then work, and was at my computer and ready to go by 8:25. I couldn't wait to talk to Tamiko!

Tamiko answered my FaceTime call with a big smile—and an even bigger taiyaki in her hands! She was wearing a frilly white babydoll dress that looked like she'd stolen it from a little kid in the 1800s. Plus, she had fixed her shiny dark hair in two long braids. She looked kooky and trendy and adorable.

"Alley Cat!" she shouted, holding the taiyaki aloft toward the camera. "Look what I'm about to eat for dessert! Are you jealous?"

I laughed and felt so excited to see Tamiko again that I was speechless. I missed her so much and was giddy at this proof of her existence, and her sameness, even if she was on the other side of the earth and fourteen hours ahead of me.

The treat looked yummy too. Taiyaki was a hollow, fish-shaped cake, and recently it had become popular to use it as an ice cream cone. The ice cream was scooped into the open mouth of the fish, and you held the fish around the tail while you ate the ice cream. Tamiko was forever trying to get my mom to sell them at Molly's, but it was a lot of work to bake the taiyaki.

Tamiko took a big bite. "I'm telling you—we have to figure out a way to start serving these at Molly's. I know we'd sell out every day!"

I laughed. Tamiko was just the same as always: dressed in a quirky outfit, enthusiastic about her little obsessions, opinionated and kind of a know-it-all, in a good way.

"Well, it definitely looks more appetizing then the cold cereal I had for breakfast," I said, finally finding my voice.

Tamiko laughed. "Oh, that's right. I forgot about

the time difference. Good morning to you! So what's up? Fill me in. What's new?"

I hesitated. "Nothing really. I just miss you a lot."

"Aww, I miss you guys too," Tamiko said. "How's everything going at Molly's? How's Sierra?"

"Everything's fine," I said. "And Sierra's . . . Sierra."

"Uh-oh," Tamiko said. "What does *that* mean?"

I sighed. "Nothing's wrong. Really. It's just . . ." I hesitated, and then just blurted it out in one long surge. "Remember how we were talking about how perky she is? How she can't go five minutes without making a new friend? Does it ever seem to you like life is so much easier for Sierra? I'm not even really sure how to explain what I mean. It's just—" But before I could finish my sentence, Tamiko interrupted me.

"You mean sweet, pretty, talented, sunshiny Sierra? The one who everyone likes and who is always in a good mood?" Tamiko took another bite of taiyaki. "Of course I've noticed! How could you not? She's like a constant ray of sunshine at Molly's." Tamiko paused for a second. Then she leaned toward the screen and said in a low voice, "It gets on my nerves sometimes, if you want to know the truth."

I felt a rush of relief. "I've been feeling that way

lately, and also feeling crummy about myself in comparison. I don't know how to handle it," I said. "What do I do?"

Tamiko shrugged. "There's nothing to 'do.' That's Sierra! That's the way she is! That's what we love about her, even though she can drive us crazy sometimes. You can't change your best friends. And anyway, why would you want to?"

I gulped. "I just wish maybe *I* could be a little more Sierra-like," I said. "Not all the time, but once in a while, maybe."

Tamiko considered this while taking another bite of her taiyaki. "Well, that's something for you to figure out. It has nothing to do with Sierra."

I sighed. "That's basically what my mom said too."

"Look, you do you," Tamiko said. "You know? That's all I can say! People always like you when you give them a chance, Alley Cat. You just need to put yourself out there. Get your writerly funk *on*, girl! Hey, speaking of writing, I sent you guys a bunch of postcards—but they'll probably get to you way after I'm already home!"

I laughed. "I'll look forward to reading them anyway. I love postcards."

Suddenly I heard my mom calling me. "Allie, I'm leaving! I don't want to get to Molly's too late! Do you need a ride to the Y?"

Reluctantly I thanked Tamiko and we ended the call, blowing kisses and counting the days until her return. Between *you do you*, *put yourself out there*, and something about getting my *writerly funk on*, Tamiko had given me a lot to think about.

At writing class later that morning, Taylor, Sam, and Anika were chatting away when I entered. I smiled and even mustered a little hello for them, and they smiled and waved, but I was too shy to walk over and join them. (Sorry, Tamiko—this was me doing me!) I sat down at my desk and pulled out my piece. I had only increased it to four hundred words before I'd run out of energy the night before, and now, in order to seem busy, I looked it over as if it fascinated me.

I was hugely relieved when, moments later, Ms. Gallo swirled through the door in a breezy skirt and tank top, calling out greetings. She unpacked her bag onto her desk and chattered away. I looked forward to the start of the class so that the pressure to socialize would go away.

Finally Ms. Gallo perched on her desk, looked at her watch, and clapped her hands. "All right. Let's get started, writers! Who had fun doing this assignment?"

I watched to see who raised their hands, and when I saw it was everyone, I raised mine, too. I didn't want to be the only one, for fear of getting called on.

"Wonderful!" she said. "Who would like to share theirs first?"

Everyone's hands dropped at once.

"Come on, folks! This is a workshop. Everyone will have to share sooner or later. It's easier to go first, I promise," she said with a winning smile.

Two or three hands reluctantly lifted. Needless to say, mine was not one of them.

"Sam, right? Thanks for volunteering. Ready?" she asked.

He nodded and began to read. He was an amazing writer, and his vocabulary was awesome. He described the food and the atmosphere at Dirt Treats, and his description of the Amazing UnBurger in particular was incredibly detailed. He went into all sorts of references from vegetarian food experts, and he gave quotes from the people at the truck. Also, he'd returned for two more visits—for both lunch and dinner on Wednesday—and he compared the different things he'd tried, as well as the things he'd tried repeatedly. I was so blown away by his piece that I think my jaw was actually hanging open. There was NO WAY I'd ever read a piece in the class now. NO WAY!

When he finished, there was ecstatic clapping from the class, and Ms. Gallo said, "Wow! That was so well done, Sam. You did major research, and your writing is gorgeous. I'm impressed. Now, what we usually do in a workshop is go around the room and have each person give a compliment to the author and then a tip for improvement. Because there are sixteen of us here, I think we'll just go with four people. Otherwise it will take too long. Okay?"

I liked the way Ms. Gallo referred to Sam as "the author." That was cool. But I was not about to volunteer to criticize anything Sam had written. I thought it was perfect, and anyway, it really wasn't my place to give advice to such a good writer. Plus, I'd written about the same topic, and mine wasn't nearly as good or as long. Anything I said would just sound like sour grapes.

Taylor volunteered to critique first. He noted that

Sam's adjectives throughout were very effective and strong, making Taylor's senses come alive as he listened. Sam smiled. It was a really nice compliment. For his tip, Taylor said to maybe give more description of who the experts were that Sam was quoting, since he didn't know them and wasn't sure why he should trust them. Sam nodded in agreement and made a note in his notebook. I smiled at Taylor. What he'd said was good. A couple of other kids went, and their compliments were huge while their advice was tiny.

"Come on, writers, don't be shy with your tips!" counseled Ms. Gallo. "Learning to look critically at writing will help your own writing as well as the person you're critiquing. It's community service! It's the gift that keeps on giving! Now, who wants to read next?" She scanned the room, and her eyes alighted on me. "Would you like to go next, my M. J. Connor friend? What's your name again?"

I nearly died on the spot. My cheeks started to burn as I shook my head. "I'm Allie. And, uh, I wrote about the same exact thing as Sam, so it would probably be, uh, better to have someone else go?" Just getting the words out with all those eyes upon me was torture.

Ms. Gallo smiled encouragingly at me. "I think that would make it even *more* interesting! Why don't you give it a shot? Don't be nervous. Just pretend we're not here."

Oh jeez. Was it that obvious that I was nervous? "Uh, okay." I gulped, trying to channel Tamiko's advice to get my writerly funk on, whatever that meant!

My hands shook as I lifted the paper and began to read.

"A little louder, please," said Ms. Gallo kindly.

I lifted my voice, and it wobbled a little. I was so nervous while I was reading that I kind of had an out-of-body experience, like this was happening to someone else. It was over before I knew it, and I remembered exactly none of it. I sat perfectly still, my face aflame, waiting for (dreading) the feedback.

"That was wonderful, Allie," said Ms. Gallo. "A little short, though. Is it the full five hundred words?"

I shook my head. "I only came up with four hundred," I said softly.

She nodded. "Okay. My compliment is that I liked the way you described the eco aspect as part of your review. It was well done and relevant, and a good slant. My criticism is, it could be longer. I wanted more. Who wants to give the next critique?"

I nodded at Ms. Gallo and, with shaking hands, made a note of her critique in my notebook.

One girl said my description of the Amazing UnBurger made her mouth water, and other people agreed, which made me feel really good. Another said she liked my attention to detail on the food I had tried, but she wished I'd gone into more depth about other offerings on the menu besides what I'd eaten. Many people agreed with that, which made me cringe because it was true—I should have done that. Another person said he would have liked it if I had criticized something. Then he would have known it wasn't just a puff piece full of compliments, and he would have trusted me more. Everyone began to chatter away about how much a reviewer should criticize versus how much they should praise, and I sat back and let the din pass over my head as people ripped my piece to shreds, or so it felt.

Ugh.

The criticisms felt more specific and real to me than the compliments; I knew I'd remember them forever and toss and turn in bed that night, thinking back on class and the changes I wished I'd made. I wasn't sure I had the nerves for this level of public humiliation.

Finally Ms. Gallo clapped her hands once to get everyone's attention. "All right. This piece has been fantastic for us because it's given us a great springboard from which to deconstruct a restaurant review and cover the conventions of the form. Thank you, Allie, for sharing with us." She went up to the board with her marker. "Now let's list all the components of a restaurant review. . . ."

As all the kids in the class engaged in vigorous debate, everyone speaking, energized, interested, I let the nerves in my body settle. I felt wrung out, like I'd just run a marathon. My muscles relaxed from their tension. My red face calmed and went back to a normal color and temperature. My sweaty palms dried up, and I began to breathe at a regular pace.

I didn't want to read in class ever again. I wasn't a good enough writer, and I hated being the center of attention. It was just awful. I planned to sit in the back row for the rest of the classes and keep my mouth shut. I felt I'd earned a rest after being so mortified.

But then something funny happened during the break.

I stood up to go eat my granola bar in the bathroom, but I couldn't move because all the kids in the class were suddenly swarming me. They peppered me with comments and questions.

"Hey, that was so awesome, that talk that your piece kicked off. . . ."

"Where are you going to write about next?"

"You were so brave to read your piece. I just could never . . ."

"Did you really think the radishes were good? I just couldn't even bring myself to try them. . . ."

"Which M. J. Connor piece should I read first?"

There was nothing for me to do but reply to everyone. Pretty soon, I opened my granola bar and just ate it while we all chatted. I never even made it to the bathroom. It was the strangest thing, but these kids were all acting like we were friends or something.

When Ms. Gallo called the class back to order, a girl leaned over from her desk and, gesturing to herself and her friend, whispered, "Let's go to the next place together, okay?"

I nodded and sat back down at my desk.

What on earth had just happened? Was this me doing me, as Tamiko had advised?

The rest of the class flew by, and at the end the two girls walked out with me. Their names were Jeanie and Marina, and we made a plan to check out a new Korean hot chicken place together over the weekend.

I practically floated to work after that. I couldn't wait to share my news with Sierra. She'd be so excited for me! Except, when I reached Molly's . . . she wasn't behind the counter, even though she was supposed to be there fifteen minutes before me.

I waved at Rashid, the college kid at the counter, ran to my mom's office, and flung open the door to share the news about making new friends. But she wasn't there either. Where *was* everybody when I needed them?

CHAPTER SEVEN

I'M JEALOUS OF MY BFF

Rashid headed off duty as I washed up behind the counter and put on my apron. Sierra had still not arrived. Her chronic tardiness had gotten so bad this year that my mom had asked her to come in fifteen minutes before her shift, just to be sure she was ready. Sierra had gotten a lot better, but since summer had begun, it seemed like she was backsliding. It was five minutes past the hour, which made her twenty minutes late. I was dying to tell her my news, so it made the minutes pass even more slowly.

People started coming in for their after-lunch ice creams, and a small line had formed when Sierra finally bounded in twenty-five minutes late, with a huge smile and her three other band members in tow.

"Ali-li! Sorry I'm late! We just cut an amazing new track!" she cried, but she didn't seem sorry at all. Her friends all got in line for ice cream, doubling the number of people who needed to be waited on, and Sierra went straight to the music system to attach her phone before even taking care of our customers.

My blood started to boil.

"Sierra!" I hissed. "Forget the music. We need to help the customers, *now*!"

She looked up and smiled at the people in line. "Just wait till you hear this new song, everyone! We just recorded the final version. It's called 'Peppermint Park' and it will make your ice cream taste even more delicious, I promise!"

The people in line laughed, but I stared daggers at Sierra, then turned back to keep working, which was what we were there for.

"This isn't *America's Got Talent*, you know," I spat as Sierra finished washing up and joined me at the ice cream counter.

"I love how you kids have created this cool music scene in here!" said one of the customers as he paid me.

I grimaced and nodded my head rigidly. "Thanks," I said through gritted teeth.

My mom arrived, finally, and I was too busy and honestly too cranky now to go tell her my news.

"Hello, girls! Love the upbeat music!" she trilled as she passed through to her office in the back.

Grrr! Not her, too!

"Hey, Sierra!" called one of Sierra's friends from a café table in the front. "Turn it up!"

Sierra made a move to turn up the music, but I stopped her. "No!" I said firmly. "This is not a club! We have little kids in here!"

Sierra looked around the store innocently. "Where?"

"Well . . . not right now. But we will, soon!"

Sierra gave me a funny wide-eyed look that seemed to say, *O-kaaaaay, weirdo*. But she moved away from the speakers and went to take an order from a mom with two little girls who had thankfully just walked in and proved me right.

I was washing milkshake-mixing cups while Sierra got two hot fudge sundaes and a vanilla milkshake for the family. They were just about to sit down at a table when one of the girls dropped the tray, sending the ice cream everywhere. The little girls immediately burst into tears.

But Sierra handled everything with her usual sunny

personality. She had everything cleaned up as quick as a flash, and she promised the children that their new sundaes would be even bigger and better than the ones the girl had dropped. After Sierra made the new order and delivered it to their table, she gave each girl an extra sprinkle of happy. They blinked through their tears and smiled adoringly at Sierra.

"You're a miracle worker!" the mom exclaimed.

For some reason all this made me even grumpier than usual. Sierra wiped up all the tables and did some sweeping, all while humming happily. I stewed silently for a while as I smashed Oreos on the back counter. By then we were in a lull. The shop was quiet and empty, and the humming was making me insane!

"*Must* you do that?" I blurted.

"Do what?" Sierra asked, genuinely confused.

"Hum! You've been humming for the past fifteen minutes."

"Oh, I'm sorry," Sierra said. "I honestly didn't notice. And anyway, I never knew it bothered you. I remember Tamiko commenting a while back, but you've never said anything."

"Well, it *does*," I said. I wanted to say so much more, but I bit my lip.

We worked for the next few minutes in stony silence. It was Sierra who spoke up first.

"Allie, what is it?" she asked softly.

"What is it?" I repeated. I hemmed and hawed for a second; then I decided to just go for it. "I'll tell you what it is. It's your humming. And your hugs. And your smiles. And your songs. And your band friends in here all the time. It's the Sierra show all the time. It's all about you!" Before I could stop myself, I blurted out, "It's everything I'm not! I'm taking a break—right now!"

And I ripped off my apron and rushed to the back.

I pretended to my mom that I'd taken a break to tell her about the new friends I'd made at my food-writing class. I felt glum, though. All of my excitement at my news had evaporated after Sierra had arrived with her posse. My Korean hot chicken plans seemed so pathetic compared to Sierra's legions of rocker friends who were always following her around and recording new "tracks" and filling up our shop.

"Well, I'm happy for you about your plans with your new friends," said my mom brightly. But then she paused and looked at me thoughtfully. She knew something was wrong. "Have you thought about bringing your literary influence to Molly's?"

"Yeah. Sort of. I just need to do it. I haven't been really motivated."

"Why don't you go create a book and ice cream pairing right now?" she suggested.

"Yeah." I just sat there, though.

"You know, you have to go back out there sometime," said my mom after a minute.

"I know," I said. "Skyping made me miss Tamiko so much again. It's just different without her here as a buffer if I get annoyed with Sierra. She would make a joke out of everything, and we'd all be laughing in a couple of minutes. Right now it's just awkward."

"Allie, being alone with one of your best friends shouldn't be a problem," my mom said. "I think you need to go back out there and talk to Sierra. Explain to her what you're going through. You'll feel better, I promise."

I sighed again and nodded. I retied my apron, blotted my face with a paper napkin, and took a deep breath.

The minute I got back to the counter, Sierra started talking. "Allie, what's going on?" she asked. "Please talk to me!"

I sighed. I wasn't sure where to begin. "Sierra, this is hard to say and even harder to explain, but I guess lately I've been feeling a little jealous of you."

Sierra looked shocked. "Jealous? Of ME? Why?"

I shrugged. "Maybe it's because Tamiko isn't around. When it's just you and me, it's really noticeable how easy it is for you to make friends and be around new people. It isn't like that for me. I just have you and Tamiko, and it's really hard for me to make new friends. And even to keep old ones," I added, thinking of Colin.

Sierra looked at me thoughtfully. "I wonder if it's easier for me because I have a sister? And a difficult sister at that! I'm constantly trying to think of new ways to get—and keep—her attention."

I wasn't sure. "That might have something to do with it," I said. "I know that having a messy younger brother like Tanner doesn't help me in the friend department!"

We both giggled.

"I think it's just your natural outgoingness. I don't have that at all. Plus, the stuff you're interested in is social: rock music, performing, sports, whatever. The stuff I like is more private, like reading and writing."

"Yeah, it's that introvert and extrovert thing," she said.

I bristled. "You know, I actually don't want to be called an introvert. I think it's really silly! That sixteen personalities website really upset me."

Sierra looked surprised. "Why? I thought it was so interesting."

"I felt like it was limiting. I mean, they don't know me. They don't know who I'm going to become. Why should I let them tell me who I am?"

"Huh," said Sierra. "I never really thought of it that way. I've actually been resigned to the fact that I'm just a messy, giggly social butterfly who can't settle down to anything. It was kind of bumming me out!"

I burst out laughing. "Sierra! Seriously? That's awful!"

She started to laugh too. "I know! I never even considered that it might not be right."

"There are waaaaay more than sixteen personalities, that's for sure. Nothing is one-size-fits-all!"

Sierra let out a sigh of relief. "I feel so much better! Thanks, Allie!"

"Glad to be of service," I said, still smiling.

Sierra grew serious. "But, Allie, I think you *can* share your reading and writing. It doesn't have to be private. I was at a café with my mom the other day, and they had a poem of the day on the blackboard. You could totally do that here!" she said, gesturing to the blackboard we used for specials. "You could write your own or share a famous one. Every day!"

"That's a good idea, actually," I said. "I've also been meaning to bring back the book and ice cream pairings I started in the school newspaper. I kind of let that slip after I got back from camp."

Sierra was nodding. "You know so much about books and literature. You've got to share it with the world!"

Her enthusiasm was contagious. "Thanks!" I said, feeling much better. "I just get shy about things, you know?"

"Think of yourself as thoughtful instead of shy. I read that somewhere. Not that it really applies to me, but the idea is to rethink things that bug you about yourself and see them as positive. It's a thing!"

I nodded. "By the way, I really wanted to tell you that I made a plan for this weekend with two girls from my writing class. I knew you'd be proud of me."

"Oh, Ali-li, I am! Way to go! What are you going to do with them?"

I filled Sierra in and even invited her, but she declined, and I was a tiny bit glad. If she had come, I would have leaned on her and let her run the whole outing, and it wouldn't have been good for me, even though it would have made me less nervous.

"It's really cool that you're making writer friends. It's fun to have friends who share your interests."

"Thanks," I said. "I learned from the master." I did a little bow to her.

"It has been really cool getting to know all those music kids from band camp," she agreed. "Plus, the Wildflowers have added a lot to my life."

"I know," I said. "I've been feeling kind of jealous of all those rocker friends of yours. They're pretty intimidating. Some of them have blue hair and are way cooler than I could ever dream of being." I laughed, but it was really to mask how I felt.

"Don't be silly, Allie. You're as cool as anyone. You know yourself, and you don't change to accommodate trends or act like a chameleon just to fit in with a group. THAT is coolness."

"Hmm," I said. I wasn't sure.

"Listen," she said. "I have an idea. I'm going to a Wildflowers rehearsal after work today. Do you want to come with me?"

"Why? I can't sing or play an instrument! Just when I'm starting to feel better about myself, you want me to feel worse?" I joked as I snapped a dish-cloth at her.

"No, silly," Sierra said. "Just come, hang out with all of us, the other girls. You'll see that the rock-ers aren't intimidating and that making new friends isn't that difficult. I think you're being too hard on yourself."

"Okay," I said grudgingly.

Sierra gave me a big hug. "And remember," she said, "none of them will ever be my besties like you and Tamiko! We are BFFs forever! Remember that!"

"I'll try," I agreed as I hugged Sierra back. "This hug is a good reminder!"

CHAPTER EIGHT

HANGING OUT WITH THE WILDFLOWERS

When the afternoon settled into a lull, I took a wet cloth and wiped the chalkboard clean. Without Tamiko there to create her spontaneous specials, the board had been sitting empty anyway. It was time for some poetry!

I wanted to find a poem that referenced one of our best-selling ice cream flavors. I scrolled through my phone searching for "banana poem" and "s'mores poem," but I didn't find anything too great. However, I did find a good quote from the poet Wallace Stevens. It was, "The only emperor is the emperor of ice cream." I liked that.

I took the pink chalk pen, and in my neatest cursive I wrote the quotation and attribution on the

board. It took a couple of tries, because the letters had to be big enough to be legible but small enough so that the whole quote would fit on the chalkboard. Then it had to look pretty. By the fifth try, I was satisfied, and just in time for the afternoon rush. And guess what? We got three compliments on it right away!

Sierra turned and smiled at me each time, and I felt so good.

"Ice cream and poetry, a perfect combination!" said one guy. I agreed with him wholeheartedly, and he gave me a couple of ideas for future poems, which I appreciated.

After our shift we tidied up, and I ducked into the bathroom to brush my hair and make sure I didn't have sprinkles in my teeth or anything. I was nervous to go hang out with the Wildflowers, but I knew that I needed to push myself out of my comfort zone and practice making friends.

"Go for it!" I whispered to myself. "What's the worst thing that could happen? Nothing, that's what!" I took a deep breath and smiled at my reflection in the mirror. It felt a little forced, but maybe on some

subconscious level it would help. I squared my shoulders and left the bathroom.

Back at the counter, Sierra explained that they usually practiced their songs in Reagan's garage, so that's where we were heading.

"The girls are excited that you're coming with me," Sierra said. "They want to try out some of our new songs in front you. You'll be our test audience!"

On the bus on the way to Reagan's we discussed some of the songs that Sierra was struggling with. It was a good distraction for my nervousness. Then when we entered Reagan's garage and were greeted happily by the girls, it made me feel even more relaxed. Even Tessa, who had a major crush on Colin, was kind and welcoming. In fact, she walked right over to me with a big smile and gave me a hug.

"Allie, I'm so glad you're here," she said warmly. "I know it's been a little awkward between us because of Colin." I gulped. "And I still really like him," Tessa continued. "But I realized recently that maybe he and I are just destined to be friends, and that's okay too. In fact, I wrote a song about it. Do you want to hear it?"

"Sure," I said. Anything about Tessa being "just

friends" with Colin was *destined* to become my new favorite song!

The Wildflowers all took their positions, and Reagan counted them in.

The song was called "Moving On," and it was really good. I found myself humming along with the catchy chorus and tapping my foot in time with the upbeat tempo. At the end I applauded wildly, and everyone laughed.

"It's beautiful," I said, and I meant it. "You did a really great job on that one."

Tessa smiled. "The songs come easier when they're from the heart," she said.

"So does writing," I agreed, smiling back. It seemed like Tessa and I were starting a friendship, and I liked the feeling.

Next the girls played a bunch of new songs for me to hear and comment on, including "Dear Future Crush." I took notes in my notebook as they performed, thinking of Ms. Gallo and how she liked a compliment to balance out each critique or "tip." Just like in class, I made sure to even things out and to be as specific as possible. When I read it all out loud in the end, I was very diplomatic but honest in my comments. I could tell that they all appreciated it.

Sierra had upped her game with the "Dear Future Crush" lyrics, but they still needed work. The chorus was great, but she didn't know what to talk about in the verses. I reminded her about our funny conversation with Tamiko, where we all imagined what our future crushes were doing right then and there. This got everyone inspired, and we all started floating ideas. Pretty soon we were laughing hysterically as our future crushes' lives got more and more elaborate and silly. I took notes and made sure to write down every idea that came out of everyone's mouths. You never could know what would be useful in the song or what might become the inspiration for a new song down the road.

After a while we took a break from working on Sierra's song to chat.

"Lyrics are really tough for us, except for Tessa," said Kasey, the keyboard player. "We all get great ideas and can come up with one or two verses, but then we have a hard time making a whole song out of them."

"I know what you mean," I answered. "Sometimes I start to write a poem or a short story and I feel like I don't have enough material. It can be really hard when you're trying to rhyme something. You have to kind of squeeze in the words that sound alike, and then build the poem around that. It rarely works out well, unless you're Shakespeare—"

"Or Dr. Seuss!" added Sierra.

"Yeah, but he made up a lot of his words," I said.

"It's so hard!" said Reagan with a sigh.

"Do you guys ever use a rhyming dictionary?" I asked. We'd used them in Ms. Healy's class a lot the previous year.

"No. What's that?" asked Reagan.

"You can find them online—or they even publish book versions. You just look up a word you're trying to rhyme, and it lists all the possibilities. Plus, if you use the online version, you can check the meanings of the words it suggests too. Then you can be sure your lyrics are making sense."

Tessa was typing on her phone. "Cool! I've got a website here. This is awesome! Thanks, Allie." She grinned at me.

"No prob!" I grinned back.

"I also like the way you gave a compliment, then a criticism, when you were discussing our songs, Allie," said Reagan. "I think we should have that as a policy for the band. What do you think, girls? Sound good?"

Kasey was nodding. "Totally. I think it will make our songs better if we can be more honest with one another. I'm looking at you, Sierra Perez!"

Sierra laughed and blushed. "What? I don't want to hurt people's feelings! Plus, I pretty much love everything."

Tessa rolled her eyes. "We know! And every*one*!"

"Oh, Sierra!" I said. "They feel the same way as Tamiko and I do?"

"About our little social butterfly?" said Reagan, slinging an arm affectionately around Sierra's neck.

"That's what we call her too!" I said.

Sierra was laughing; she didn't mind. "I'm a people person!"

"That, you are!" agreed Kasey.

Sierra and I smiled at each other. I was happy for her that she had this other group of nice girls who "got" her like Tamiko and I did. I was surprised I didn't feel jealous, but I figured it was because they weren't territorial about Sierra at all and were so welcoming to me.

"Ready to hit it again, girls?" said Reagan.

I decided it would be a good time for me to

depart and let them get their work done. I stood up. Besides, since my mom was still working at Molly's, I had to take the bus home, and I didn't want it to get too late.

"This has been so fun and awesome. Thank you so much for letting me sit in on your session. I loved it." I felt so relaxed and comfortable that I almost hated for it to end, but I didn't want to overstay on my first time with them.

They protested and would let me go only when I promised to come back again in a week to check their lyrics progress.

Kasey helped me gather my things, and as she handed me my notebook, a piece of paper fluttered out. "Oops!" she said, bending to pick it up. Then she glanced at it as she handed it to me. "Hey! What's this?" she said. She started to read out loud,

"One is the sun—burning fiercely,
Pulling all to her side.
One is the moon—always moving,
Riding a new tide.
One is fiery gold, electric, loyal, and wild.
The other is cool, silver, bold, and styled."

I felt my cheeks grow warm as she read. "Oh, haha. It's just a poem I've been working on," I said, trying to blow it off. "I've been playing around with it, but I got stuck on a word and never finished it."

Reagan smiled as she read it over Kasey's shoulder. "Pulling all to her side," she repeated. "Gee, I wonder who that could be—SIERRA!"

Sierra was staring at the page in wonder. "You wrote a poem about me . . . and Tamiko?"

I shrugged. "You know how I've been feeling lately. Sometimes writing poetry helps."

"Ooh, now we get to help you with your poem, just like you helped us with our lyrics!" said Tessa with a smile.

"Hmm, what could be a good word describing Sierra here?" said Kasey.

"Kind?" suggested Reagan.

"Friendly?" suggested Tessa.

"Outgoing?" said Kasey.

I smiled at Sierra. "Generous. That's the word. She's fiery gold, generous, and wild. Done!"

"Love it!" said Kasey as Reagan high-fived me.

Sierra walked across the garage and gave me a huge hug. "Love ya, Alley Cat." Then she whispered into my ear. "And look, just like that . . . you have three new friends. Just by being you."

"Thanks, Sierra. Love you, too." We did a tight squeeze, and then I hugged all the Wildflowers and headed out. I'd had a great time, and I left with a feeling of warmth, calm, and confidence. And for the first time in a long time, I was actually looking forward to my next social outing—my Korean hot chicken dinner with Jeanie and Marina from class.

CHAPTER NINE

NEW FRIENDS ARE FUN

Crispy Chicken was new in town, in kind of an up-and-coming neighborhood. My mom dropped me off, and my dad would pick me up, since I was staying at his house that night.

I was the first to arrive. Because it was early, the restaurant wasn't too busy, and I scored a table. I pulled out my notebook and started taking detailed notes about the decor and atmosphere. The metal-topped tables were low, with small wooden stools that could be moved around anywhere. A sign told people that the seating was first come, first seated and asked diners to please vacate as soon as they'd finished eating, so that other people could sit. The floor of the restaurant was a light wood, as was the ceiling, and it all felt very modern and clean.

Along a counter where you could stand and eat, there were dispensers of different hot sauces, with small pleated cups to carry the sauce to your table. There were white china crocks filled with individually wrapped pairs of chopsticks, and napkin dispensers everywhere. Signs proclaimed that people needed to bus their own tables because YOUR MOM ISN'T HERE TO CLEAN UP AFTER YOU, which I thought was funny. The music was mellow hip-hop, and the people behind the counter were mostly teenagers. They seemed to be having fun together.

I made sure to jot down the entire menu, including drinks (mostly variations on iced tea), so I could refer to it in anything I wrote about the restaurant. I also noted the kinds of people who were there—mostly young people and not too many families.

It took me about ten minutes to write all this down, and when I finished, I looked at my phone. 6:08. I was so nervous that I suddenly wondered if I'd gotten the date or time wrong. But I had confirmed with Jeanie and Marina by text earlier in the day, I reminded myself. Had I gotten it wrong? Had I made a typo and set the date for the next day? I checked my phone just in case. Yup. Right time and day.

I wondered where they were. The restaurant was starting to fill up, and I wasn't going to be able to hold the table for much longer. In fact, just then a woman gestured at the table and said, "Are you using all these seats?"

I shrugged. "I think so. Well, three of them. You can have the fourth?"

She shook her head. "No, I need two. Thanks." And she wandered away. I felt embarrassed. 6:13. Should I call them? My imagination started going wild. Were they standing me up? Were we really even friends? Was this a . . . prank? I craned my head all around to see if they might be here, watching me and laughing, but no.

Stop, Allie. You're being paranoid, I told myself. I looked at my phone. 6:15. *Should I just call my dad to come get me now?* My stomach clenched in embarrassment. As I gripped my phone and stared at it, it suddenly rang.

"Allie! Oh my gosh, I'm so glad I reached you! It's Jeanie. Listen. . . ." She was all out of breath and talking fast. "Marina's mom had a fender bender on her way here—"

I gasped. "Oh no! Is everyone okay?"

"Yes. It's fine, and it wasn't her fault, and no one was hurt, thank goodness. But we realized she was going to be there for a long time waiting to do the police report. We were finally able to leave, so now we're walking . . . and we're about . . . Marina, how much farther?"

"Six blocks," came the muffled reply in the background.

"We're six blocks away. We're so sorry we're late. We couldn't call sooner because there was all this drama. Anyway, we'll be there soon. Okay? You probably thought we stood you up! I'm so sorry!"

"Oh, haha, well . . . ," I said. "See you soon." We hung up.

I took a deep breath. "Okay," I said out loud to myself. "Phew."

I was embarrassed now that I'd been so paranoid. I'd even imagined they were spying on me to watch me squirm. That was ridiculous! I really needed to calm down when it came to friends. (My mind flashed back to the sixteen personalities diagnosis, where it said that the Logistician saw dependency on others as a weakness! They often unreasonably blamed themselves for things that weren't their fault!)

Minutes later (after I'd turned away three more groups of people looking to sit), Jeanie and Marina burst into Crispy Chicken. I saw them scan the crowd and then point to me and rush across the restaurant—or try to—and then finally reach my table.

"Allie! We are so sorry! We never meant to be so late!" said Marina in a high state of anxiety.

"We were going to be early so you wouldn't have to wait for us alone!" said Jeanie breathlessly.

They collapsed onto their stools and breathed heavily.

"Please don't worry. It's fine! Just catch your breath. I've been people-watching and taking notes for my piece. Are you sure everything is okay with your mom and the car? We can do this another time if that's better for you guys."

"No way!" Marina cried. "I was looking forward to this so much, I wouldn't miss it for anything!"

I beamed, flattered. "Now, we need to order right away. We can take turns ordering, and I can go first. Or maybe I can order for all of us while you two catch your breath—and you can just pay me back. Otherwise we'll lose the table. Okay?"

"Totally. It smells amazing in here!" said Jeanie,

her eyes bright with excitement.

"I'm going to go up and look at the menu. I'll be right back," said Marina.

Soon we had our orders in, and then our number was called and Jeanie went to claim the food. She returned to our table bearing the tray aloft like she was carrying a crown to present to a queen.

"Ta-da!" she cried, lowering the tray onto the table. On it were three baskets of fried chicken parts, two sides of kimchi, and a small bowl of pickled radish and cucumber.

"Yum!" I agreed.

Jeanie and I handed the food around while Marina doled out the chopsticks and napkins, and we tucked in. I was suddenly starving.

The three of us fell silent at first as we attacked our chicken. It was incredible! And also super-spicy! Wow!

It was like nothing I'd had before. On the outside they'd drizzled a light, sweetish, spicy sauce that was sticky. The crust was so crispy that it shattered when I bit into it. It was thin and light. The chicken meat was juicy and salty. The chicken was super-messy to eat, mostly because of the sauce, but not greasy at all.

I think I went through about twenty napkins!

Coming up for air, I tried the kimchi and then the pickles. The kimchi was also spicy and very sour, which was a good contrast to the chicken skin. The pickles were sweetish and sour, and very cold, but most of all, delicious.

"I need more!" said Jeanie.

We burst out laughing, but we all agreed. The first time, we had ordered just drumsticks and wings, but this time we tried the thighs, and I liked them even better. There were a lot of other things on the menu, but we were starting to get full.

"Do we have to order the other stuff?" I groaned.

Jeanie shook her head. "I think we can just review the chicken. If you say up front that it's the review of just one dish and not a restaurant review, you won't have to cover everything."

"We will have to come back and try the chicken again, though, just to be fair," said Marina with a laugh.

We sat back, satisfied and sticky, and we each gave a deep, contented sigh.

"Do they have dessert?" Marina craned her head to see.

"They have some kind of lemon ice. That's all," I remembered. "What do you guys think?"

"Anyone want one?" asked Marina.

Jeanie and I both shook our heads. "I don't have another inch to spare," I said, patting my stomach.

"I'll get one to go," said Marina, "and we can walk off this food for a bit."

"Look, there's someone who needs our table," said Jeanie as Marina headed off. It was a woman struggling with two small boys and a heavily laden tray. "Yoo-hoo! Over here!" Jeanie waved as I hurriedly stood and wiped down our table.

Jeanie dodged through the crowd to help the lady with her tray, and as the woman looked up, I saw that it was Ms. Healy, my favorite teacher!

She was smiling gratefully at Jeanie and shepherding the boys to our table.

"Allie! What a treat! How are you, sweetheart?" Ms. Healy gave me a big hug. "How's your summer? These are my nephews, Bradley and Timmy. They're just visiting me. Say hello, boys, to my star student, Allie."

The boys were adorable and turned to me to solemnly say hello. Inside I was bursting from the "star student" compliment.

"Thank you so much for the table. I was desperate back there," continued Ms. Healy as she settled her nephews onto their stools. She asked me how my summer was going and what I was reading, and how the food was.

I explained that we were there to review the food for our food-writing class, and Ms. Healy got super-excited. "Oh, Allie, I'm so glad you're taking that class! You're such a fantastic writer. I see a real future for you in the world of writing!"

I felt warm and happy from the additional compliment. "Thank you so much."

"Thank you for the table and for the help getting over here! You have such nice friends. Just like you!"

We chatted for another minute and then said goodbye, and Jeanie and I went to meet Marina outside.

Marina was finishing the dregs of her lemon ice. "You girls sure you don't want to try it? It's really good. Like frozen lemonade. What took you so long in there?"

"Allie ran into her English teacher, who was raving about her," Jeanie said cheerfully.

"Oh, please. She'd say that stuff about anyone." I waved my hand to dismiss it.

Jeanie put her hand on my arm. "Allie, seriously. She was raving about you. You must be really talented."

I couldn't help but smile. "Thanks. English is my favorite subject. Plus, I always like to make friends with the teacher."

"Me too," agreed Jeanie.

"Me three!" said Marina.

We all grinned at one another and then set off on a short stroll up and down the streets, window-shopping until it was time to meet our parents for our rides home. We talked the whole time about our favorite books and characters, our favorite settings, and the best poems we could think of. I'd never had friends who loved reading and writing as much as I did, and I felt cozy and happy, like I was being buoyed along in a sea of warm maple syrup, as we walked and talked and talked.

"You know what I wish right now?" said Jeanie. "I know just a few minutes ago I was stuffed, but right now I wish we were at that amazing new ice cream place, Molly's. I could demolish a mermaid sundae."

"Oh my gosh! I am obsessed with that place!" agreed Marina. "Allie, have you been yet?"

I started laughing so hard! "You guys!" I gasped. "I work there. It's my mom's ice cream parlor!"

Jeanie and Marina could not get over their shock. "Whaaaat? You are so lucky!" they squealed, and then they wanted to go over each and every flavor and how they liked them and why, as we walked all the way back to Crispy Chicken.

We hugged good-bye outside the restaurant.

"And we need an outing to Molly's ASAP!" said Marina.

"See you in class, but text me if you want to chat in the meantime!" said Jeanie with a wave as she got into her car.

I got into my dad's car and closed the door. With a happy sigh and a smile that lingered on my face, I pulled on my seat belt and clicked it into place.

"Good time?" asked my dad, already knowing the answer.

"Not a good time . . . a great time!" I said.

I was so overjoyed that I could hardly sit still in my seat. Making new friends felt amazing!

CHAPTER TEN

TEXTING COLIN

Sunday was absolute madness at Molly's. Sierra and I were so swamped after lunch that we had to get my mom to come up front and help us.

"I miss Tamiko!" I cried as I rushed past Sierra behind the counter.

"Thanks a lot!" said my mom with a laugh. She was trying to construct a mermaid sundae (one of Tamiko's signature concoctions) and kind of failing.

When things slowed down midafternoon, Sierra and I looked through the series of selfies that Tamiko had sent us the night before. It showed her trying all different flavors of soft cream ice cream, and the photos displayed a rainbow of unusual ice cream colors. Matcha! said the first pic, and it showed Tamiko eating green ice cream. The next photo showed her in a different outfit eating black ice cream. (Kuro-goma: Black Sesame! it said.) Then a purple dollop of soft serve (Beni-Imo: Purple Sweet Potato, yum yum!), an orange one (Mikan: Mandarin Orange!), gray (Volcanic Ash Vanilla: Say whaaaaat?), tan (Soy Sauce and Miso . . . faves so far), and more.

I wish I could bring these back for you! said the last photo.

"I miss our girl." I sighed.

"Me too," agreed Sierra.

Next, I took a few minutes to create a book and ice cream pairing. To restart the tradition, I knew I wanted to go with a classic—my favorite book, *Anne of Green Gables*. One of Anne's favorite things is strawberries, so it was only natural that I'd pair the book with our famous Balsamic Strawberry ice cream. I put a little blurb on the board that said, "If you haven't read *Anne of Green Gables*, it's time to pick it up and warm your heart. Then cool down with some Balsamic Strawberry ice cream, featuring Anne's most favorite fruit." Then I added a little quotation from the book that said, "Dear old world . . . you are very lovely, and I am glad to be alive in you."

"That looks so nice," said Sierra as she paused to read it. "It's so Molly's!"

Her compliment warmed *my* heart, but not as much as when Mrs. O'Brien came in for ice cream later. She owned the bookstore at the mall and coordinated the Book Fest celebration at my old school.

"Allie! Hello! How was camp?" she asked with a smile when she reached the counter.

"Hi, Mrs. O'Brien. It was awesome. Never enough time for reading, but still great."

"Wonderful! And how did you like the books you picked out?"

"I loved them," I said.

She was nodding. "Good. I have some new recommendations for you when you come in next. Now, what have we here?" she asked, putting on the reading glasses that had been perched on her head. She studied my book pairing and smiled.

"As a huge Anne fan, I simply must try the ice cream that goes with the book. Could I please have a Balsamic Strawberry scoop in a cone?"

"Coming right up!" I said.

I busied myself with the ice cream and presented it to Mrs. O'Brien with a big flourish.

She tried it. "Mmmm. Wow! This is amazing. What a combination. Tart, sour, creamy, just the right amount of sweet. It's a revelation!"

I grinned. "A lot of my mom's flavors are pretty unconventional—that's what she calls them—but they really give you 'scope for imagination,'" I said, quoting a trademark snippet from *Anne of Green Gables*.

"The world 'wouldn't be half so interesting if we know all about everything, would it?'" replied Mrs. O'Brien in another Anne quotation, and we both laughed. "You know, Allie, I have an idea. Maybe you'd like to give me a book and ice cream pairing to feature at my store each week, and I could have it in a little frame on the counter, with the Molly's address and info. If you could list my store on your pairing sign, we'd be cross-promoting!"

I beamed. "That's such a good idea. I have to check with my mom, but I'm sure she'll say yes. She loves your store too."

Mrs. O'Brien dug into her purse and withdrew a business card and handed it to me. "Why don't you e-mail me and let me know? Then you could e-mail me a flyer each week that I can print out and feature. Sound good?"

"Great! Thank you so much."

We said our good-byes, and I was still smiling when she left.

Sierra came out from cleaning the bathroom and saw me at the counter.

"Did Colin come in and I missed it?" she asked.

I shook myself out of my daydream. "No! Why?"

"You have that dreamy grin on your face that you sometimes get. . . ."

I chuckled. "I guess it's just my happy face. But now that I think of Colin, it's my sad face!" I made a frown. "What am I going to do about him? I'm paralyzed!"

Sierra blew out a gust of air in exasperation. "Just text him! I've been telling you for weeks to contact him. What on earth are you thinking?" Her mouth was pressed into a grim line. "You're making me wonder if *I'd* even have heard from you if I hadn't marked down the date of your return from Holly Oaks and texted you the second I woke up that day. Would you have contacted me to let me know you were home?"

"Oh, Sierra, of course I would have!" I protested.

Sierra shrugged. "How can I be sure?"

I bit my lip. "I *would* have. That's how. We're friends, and you can always count on me."

"Colin probably would have thought the same thing about you about six weeks ago, Alley Cat," Sierra said quietly.

"Hmm," I said, biting on my thumbnail.

"Think about it," Sierra said.

Then my phone buzzed. It was Tamiko FaceTiming me!

In my surprise, I grappled with my phone and struggled to answer it, almost losing the call. Normally I would never pick up the phone while working, but our shift was ending in five minutes and no one was in the store.

"Tamiko!"

"Alley Cat!" she cried. "Hi!"

Sierra flew to my side. "Hi, Miko!"

"Sierra! My homies, all together!"

"We're just about finishing up at work," I said.

Tamiko laughed. "And look at me! I'm in bed!" she said as she spun her phone to show us her bed. I caught a glimpse of a low futon on the floor. "I woke up early and had some time, so I decided to call. What's going on over there?"

At that, Sierra grabbed my phone. "We were just talking about Colin," she said.

"Sierra!" I yelled.

"Talk some sense into this girl, please," Sierra said to Tamiko. "Allie's making new friends, but she's not working to keep one of her best friends of all. She's been neglecting Colin ever since she got home. She hasn't contacted him once, and when she runs into him, it's super-awkward!"

"Put her back on!" demanded Tamiko.

Sierra thrust the phone back at me.

"What?" I said sullenly. I didn't need my best friend to call me all the way from Japan to yell at me.

"Listen, old friends are gold, but new friends are important and fun too. Got me? You need to call Colin and make it up to him. This is unacceptable, Allie. How can Sierra and I help but wonder if you'll do this to us one day too? Sheesh!"

"It's different!" I wailed.

"No, it's not. Shape up or ship out, Shear!"

I had to laugh. "Ship out of where?"

Tamiko spluttered for a second. Then she laughed too. "Oh, I don't know. My grandpa has me watching too many old war movies with him! I'm just saying.

Fix this. It's good for you. Okay? And then maybe I will bring you back a nice present when I return."

"You're talking about your return already? I joked.

"You know you're counting the days!" Tamiko wagged a finger at me.

"I can't wait," I said seriously.

"Me neither!" shouted Sierra over my shoulder.

"Okay. In the meantime, get in touch with Colin. You'd better get cracking!"

I laughed. "Thanks, Tamiko."

We signed off, and I stood there for a minute, smiling at the ghost of Tamiko on my phone.

Finally Sierra said, "So?"

I sighed heavily. "So."

"Just do it. Ask him to meet you. Do it now and get it over with."

Without thinking, I took a deep breath and let my fingers fly over the keyboard of my phone.

Hi, Colin. I'm sorry I've been such a bad friend these past couple of weeks. I hope things are good with you. Are you free on Tuesday to go to Crispy Chicken with me for dinner at 6:00? Just LMK. Thanks.

I reread it only once, and then, instead of agonizing over it, I quickly pushed send.

My heart lurched and I gasped, but there was no taking it back now.

"Done?" asked Sierra.

"Done," I said. "For better or for worse." I tried to summon the courage of Anne of Green Gables, who said: "Next to trying and winning, the best thing is trying and failing." Hmmm. I wasn't so sure about that.

CHAPTER ELEVEN

A SURPRISE VISITOR

To say that I checked my phone five hundred times over the course of the next day would be . . . an understatement.

Colin did not reply.

By the time I went to bed on Monday night (after answering ten question mark texts from Sierra with big fat NOs), I had moved through the whole spectrum of emotions, from mortified, to anxious, to furious, to sad, to angry, and back, multiple times. I wouldn't let myself regret sending the text, though. I knew that the ball had been in my court, and I'd owed him that much, at least.

I slept fitfully and did not allow myself to check my phone until I was in the car with my mom on the way to my class at the Y. Usually the class was on Mondays and Thursdays, but Ms. Gallo had made a change this week because she had a conflict.

I looked at my phone again. Still nothing. I sighed.

"Everything okay, sweetheart?" she asked.

"Ugh," I said.

"How so?" she prodded.

I explained that I was loving my new class and had made two good friends there, in addition to the Wildflowers. But then I confessed.

"I've been a bad friend," I said, and I explained about Colin.

"So, wait, *why* didn't you contact him when you got home?" My mom was confused.

"Because I kind of like him and I thought he liked me back, and I thought he'd, like, magically and romantically know I was home, and he'd show up with a bouquet of flowers and sweep me off my feet—"

My mom was laughing. "Maybe he thought the same about you!" she interjected.

"Haha." I laughed wryly. "As if!"

"Why not? Boys have feelings too, you know!"

"Not Tanner!" I said.

"Yes, maybe not Tanner," joked my mom. "Anyway, I'm sure that when things cool down, Colin will get back to you. Don't worry."

We'd reached the Y, and my mom idled in front as I gathered up my backpack.

"You're a good kid, Allie. Don't worry," she said lightly, but her eyes held concern.

"Thanks, Mom. Love you," I replied.

"Love you too."

I pushed the door open smoothly and walked into class with a smile. Sam said hi to me, and so did Taylor and Anika. Jeanie and Marina waved me over.

"We saved you a seat," said Jeanie.

"Thanks!"

We chatted until class started, and when Ms. Gallo called us all to order, the first item was to discuss our next assignment.

"I want you all to write about something with unexpected flavors or pairings or combinations. Something where you're outside of your comfort zone, trying things that you might not usually eat or that might gross you out normally. I want you to work to find language that can express flavors and textures without necessarily labeling them as good or bad. Does anyone have any ideas?"

Jeanie's hand shot up, the only one to do so.

"Yes, Jeanie?" said Ms. Gallo with a smile.

"Allie's mom owns Molly's Ice Cream shop. . . ."

Sixteen heads swiveled to gape at me. I smiled and nodded and looked at Ms. Gallo, who was also surprised but appeared pleased.

"I've tried some really wacky stuff there this year, like balsamic vinegar and strawberry ice cream—" Jeanie continued.

"Oh, I had that! It was insane!" interrupted Sam.

"Me too! Crazy good!" agreed Anika.

The class started chattering among themselves, and Ms. Gallo let it go for a minute.

Then she called us all to order again. "What we need is a class field trip. Each student will try a different flavor—ideally one outside your comfort zone—and write a short, two-hundred-and-fifty-word piece about it. How does a visit to Molly's next Thursday after class sound? The class fee will cover it, so you don't have to worry about money or transportation, okay?"

We all agreed we could go, and then Ms. Gallo

began a new topic, talking about distaste, and I glanced at Jeanie and smiled. "Thanks," I mouthed to her.

She grinned and nodded in reply. Then she leaned over and whispered, "Can you do Crispy Chicken again tonight? I'm dying to go back!"

I grimaced. "Talk at the break," I replied, and she nodded.

We split into groups to workshop one another's pieces for that day, and Anika and Sam were in my group. Neither of them had been to Crispy Chicken yet, but they said that after my piece, they were definitely going ASAP! I took that as a compliment, even as I made a note of some critiques they'd had (I'd used the word "crisp" too much), taking the criticism better this time than last. Probably because I felt more comfortable with them all now.

By the break, I was sure I'd have heard back from Colin.

But I hadn't.

Jeanie and Marina chattered on about their kimchi craving, while I sat silently, refreshing my phone.

"Is everything all right?" asked Marina kindly.

I sighed and knew I had to be honest. "I'm kind of in a weird situation with a good friend. Kind of a crush. And I asked him to go to Crispy Chicken with me tonight, but I haven't heard back yet."

"Oh," said Marina, nodding with a concerned look on her face.

Jeanie raised her eyebrows. "Listen. Give him until five. If you don't hear back, you can come with us. Okay?"

"Thanks," I agreed.

By five o'clock there was no word from Colin. I texted Jeanie and Marina to say I'd meet them for dinner at six. I was crushed, but after I had ignored him for multiple weeks, I knew that the treatment from Colin was no more than I deserved. My mom drove me to the restaurant and didn't ask any questions this time. She just breezed on about some new flavor ideas while I mm-hmm'd distractedly.

"Heyyy!" squealed Jeanie when I entered.

"Over here, Allie!" said Marina.

My heart lifted and I joined them at the table.

We chatted for a minute about what to order, and then I gave them my money and they went to get chicken thighs, kimchi, and pickles while I held the table.

They hadn't been gone more than thirty seconds when I heard my name.

"Allie?"

I turned. "Hi." I gulped.

"Is it okay if I sit down?" Colin asked.

"Uh, yeah, sure. Of course." I gestured at the empty seat and then glanced nervously at my friends in line. They hadn't noticed his arrival.

"I'm so sorry that I didn't reply!" Colin began. "I went backpacking with my family and didn't have any service until an hour ago."

"Oh!" I said, feeling my cheeks turning warm. I had just assumed he'd seen my text and ignored it. I hadn't even considered the possibility that he was out of town.

"I should've told you I was going backpacking," Colin continued in a quieter voice. "But I wasn't sure if I would . . . uh . . . hear from you anyway."

"I—I'm so sorry, Colin!" I spluttered. "I should've texted *you* when I returned from summer camp. But I got nervous . . . and I didn't know if *you* would care."

"Of course I'd care!" Colin said. Then he smiled at me. "So, we were both worried about the same thing for no reason?"

"Sorry," I said again.

"It's okay!" Colin laughed and raised his hand for a fist bump. "Great minds think alike?"

Blushing, I returned his fist bump. "Great minds think alike."

Then, as quickly as he had sat down, he stood back up. "I'd love to stay and eat, but I came as soon as I saw your text, and I haven't had a chance to shower yet. I also ran here, so I'm kind of sweaty." Now it was his turn to blush. "Can we reschedule dinner for another day, and I promise I'll smell nicer and look better then?"

You came straight from backpacking? Just to see me? Am I that important to you? And you look nice already! I had a thousand things to say, but instead I just smiled and nodded.

As soon as the door closed behind Colin, Jeanie and Marina raced over to the table with trays of food.

"Was that him?" Jeanie demanded.

"Why did he leave?" Marina asked. "Did everything go okay?"

"Yeah," I said slowly. I felt a silly grin spreading across my face. "I think he ran here just to see me!"

Jeanie raised a drumstick in the air. "Cheers to Allie's crush!" she declared.

Laughing, I picked up a drumstick of my own and tapped it against Jeanie's. Then I smiled at both of them. "And cheers to awesome new friends!"

CHAPTER TWELVE

TAMIKO'S BACK AND ALL IS WELL!

"Blackberry Lavender? Is that like the flower? You eat flowers?" Anika was laughing.

Tamiko nodded. "Yes, sometimes we have nasturtium petals, or candied violets to put on top. And Mrs. Shear is working on a rosebud flavor as we speak!"

Anika was shaking her head in wonder, and I laughed. "Give her a taste, Tamiko!" I suggested.

"I'm trying the Cereal Milk," Ms. Gallo was saying. "What a funny concept. I'm not into sweet cereal, so this will be an eye-opener for me."

My whole writing class was at Molly's, and Tamiko and Sierra were bustling around behind the counter to fill all the orders. Tamiko had returned only the day before, and though she'd been jet-lagged, she'd insisted on coming to work that day because our social media presence was "floundering" and she was sure we needed a new special, especially with the summer rush.

When Tamiko had arrived back in the shop, she'd done a double take at the chalkboard with my book pairing (and Mrs. O'Brien's contact info for book sales, which my mom had approved). Since the chalkboard was usually where her specials went, Tamiko was rightly taken aback for a minute. But without missing a beat, she said, "That is so cool, Ali-li! Will you please ask your mom for a new chalkboard for our specials?"

Soon she was concocting Japanese-inspired specials and photographing and posting them to social media and our website. My mom emerged from the back office. "We missed you, darling!" she said.

"I have presents for you all, and I can give them to you now that everyone's here."

Tamiko produced huge green-tea-flavored KitKats for us all (even Tanner); a *wagasa*, or paper umbrella, for my mom; Kabuki face masks for me and Sierra; and best of all, something called "*shokuhin* samples." The "samples" were plastic fake food that were hilariously realistic and kind of gross because of it. Each of us got an ice cream sundae in a parfait glass.

"I'll treasure mine," said my mom seriously.

"I also have this," said Tamiko. She dropped a small brochure onto the countertop in front of my mom.

"What's this?" asked my mom, picking up the brochure.

"My Japanese ice cream report. With photos and diagrams!"

"And receipts!" my mom said, laughing as she peeked at the clear plastic pocket at the back. "Oh, Tamiko, this is incredible! I can't wait to read it. Thank you so much!"

Now my class sat all around the shop, chatting and sighing happily. I was excited to see Tamiko and Sierra yakking away with Jeanie and Marina. I'd been nervous to introduce them, but they had all totally hit it off, of course. Sam, Taylor, and Anika and some of the other kids had also talked to my friends—some of them knew one another from other places—and the whole event felt fantastic.

I noticed that the napkin dispenser was almost empty, so I walked over to the supply cabinet to grab some more. Then my phone buzzed with a notification.

Hey, Allie! Do you want to go bowling together this Saturday? And then we can go to Crispy Chicken for dinner. What do you think?

Before I had time for the words to sink in, Sierra and Tamiko were peering into my phone. "Bowling, just the two of you? That's basically a full-fledged date!"

"Hey, no reading over my shoulder!" I protested, but I couldn't stop smiling.

"Are you in your happy place, Alley Cat?" asked Sierra.

I looked over at everyone from my class, especially Jeanie and Marina, sitting and eating ice cream together. "This is a great place for an introverted Logistician to work," I joked.

"What's a Logistician?" asked Tamiko, sounding perplexed.

"A great friend," said Sierra, giving me a squeeze. Then she said, "I have a surprise for you, Allie!" She ducked over to the sound system and pushed a few buttons. A catchy rhythm started on the speakers, and I found myself tapping my toe.

"What song is this?" I asked.

Sierra was smiling. "It's a new one by the Wildflowers. Listen!" She held a finger up in the air.

"One is the sun—burning fiercely,
Pulling all to her side.
One is the moon—always moving,
Riding a new tide.
One is fiery gold, generous, and wild.
The other is cool, silver, bold, and styled.
I am the earth,
Creative, strong, growing all the time. . . .
These friends are mine. . . ."

I clapped and laughed. "Sierra! It's my poem! And I thought of myself as the earth too! So funny!"

She nodded and grinned. "The Wildflowers loved it, so we set it to music and recorded it for you. It was Tessa's idea. They want you to come back so we can work some more on the lyrics, okay? And the song doesn't have a title yet either."

"Maybe we should add something about ice cream to the song," I said with a laugh. "Or something about sprinkles."

"Maybe you should call it 'A Sprinkle of Friendship,'" joked Tamiko.

She put her arms around me and Sierra and began dancing, doing a cancan. Sierra and I joined in, and soon my whole writing class was laughing and applauding.

"Hooray for me and my besties!" I said.

"Hooray for friends," said Sierra, giving me an extra squeeze.

I squeezed Tamiko and Sierra back. "Hooray for friends," I echoed. "And plenty of them!"

DON'T MISS BOOK 11:

ICE CREAM QUEEN

"Tamiko, you're going to be late for your first day of school!" Mom yelled up the stairs.

"COMING!" I yelled back. Mom was being unreasonable. I still had ten minutes to get to the bus stop, and I needed to upload my blog post before I left.

I'd just taken a mirror selfie of me in my back-to-school outfit: baggy ripped jeans and a white T-shirt with cartoony bright-orange carrots on it. I started typing.

And here's the winning outfit! Thanks for voting in my poll yesterday. I brought home so many cool outfits from Tokyo that I couldn't pick one.

Now I'm off to start another year of school. The

good news is that I finally have a class with my bestie, Sierra! 🤩 🤩

I started to type: The other good news is that I don't have to take art this year with Mr. Rivera. I love art, but that class bored me to tears! But I deleted it after just a few words. Before the summer started, I'd gotten into some big trouble for posting something negative on my blog that I'd just meant to be funny. So I was trying to be really careful.

Instead, I typed: If you're going back to school today too, remember to be your fabulous self, walk tall, and don't let the haters get you down! That's Tamiko's Take.

I studied the selfie, making sure I was okay with the image. My face looked too pale next to my jet-black hair, like I hadn't ever been out in the sun, and that was thanks to Mom's overenthusiastic sunscreen policies. I thought about filtering a glowy tan, but I knew I didn't have time. I quickly checked over the text for typos, and then, satisfied, I uploaded the post.

"TAMIKO!"

I tucked my phone into my backpack, slung it over my shoulder, and bounded down the stairs and into the kitchen. Dad was seated at the kitchen table, calmly drinking a cup of coffee.

"Why is everything so loud this morning?" he asked.

"Yeah, why?" parroted my older brother, Kai, who was halfway out the front door. Outside I could see a blue car idling in front of our house.

"Who's that? Are you getting a ride? Can I get one too?" I asked.

"That's Kevin, who's a senior, and no," Kai said.

"But—" I protested.

Kai closed the door behind him, and Mom ran up to me and handed me a lunch bag and a granola bar.

"You need to get to that bus stop, Tamiko," she said. "I'm bummed that you didn't get down here earlier. I made the pancakes and everything."

I glanced over at the stove, where pancakes that looked like smiling frog faces were stacked on a plate. Mom had gotten the pancake mold thingy when I was four years old, and she'd made me frog pancakes on special occasions ever since—and always on the first day of school.

"Save them and I'll microwave them tomorrow," I said.

"You're *welcome*, Tamiko," Mom said. Then she looked me up and down. "This is the outfit that your blog readers picked?"

I did a twirl. "Yup!"

Mom sighed. "I voted for the white shirt with the black jumper. That looks so cute on you."

"My readers have spoken!" I said. "Bye-eee!"

I raced out the door and jogged down to the corner bus stop. Even though it was September, the temperature still felt summery, and I was glad to be wearing the T-shirt today. When the bus came, I found a seat and drowned out the noise and took out my phone. First I checked my blog. Nine comments already! Then I texted Allie, my other bestie besides Sierra.

Have a great first day of school! Bet you can't wait to see Colin!

She texted back: You too! Bet you can't wait to see Ewan!

I felt my cheeks get hot. Served me right for teasing her about Colin. I replied with a tongue-stuck-out emoji and leaned back in my seat.

For most of my life I'd never imagined having a crush on a boy. It wasn't something I daydreamed about. And then last year I'd had art class with Ewan Kim, and he was nice and funny and definitely the best thing about that class. We'd started sort of hanging out, and when I was in Tokyo, he had texted me every day, sending me pictures of stuff in Bayville so I wouldn't feel homesick. And now I was kind of crushing on him, which felt weird and nice and scary and exciting all at the same time.

Allie texted back with another tongue-stuck-out emoji. I looked at it, and then my screensaver popped up—Grandpa Soto and me with our heads together, smiling into the camera. I'd had a blast in Tokyo, just like I did every summer. My dad was born there, and Grandpa Soto still lives there, so we visit him every year.

This year had been extra fun because I'd been on special assignment for Molly's Ice Cream, the shop owned by Allie's mom, Mrs. Shear. Sierra, Allie, and I work there on Sundays and I handle social media for the shop on the side. Mrs. Shear had given me fifty dollars to try as many flavors as I could of Japanese soft-cream ice cream, which is basically like soft-serve ice cream here in the States, except the flavors are really different. I'd tried black sesame, soybean flour, and even miso-flavored soft cream (yes, the same miso that's in the soup you get in sushi restaurants). That all may sound weird, but everything was really delicious. I couldn't wait to see if Mrs. S. was going to come up with any new flavors based on my research.

The ice cream posts had been a big hit on my blog too, but frankly, I think I could post pictures of paint drying and that would be a big hit. That's why they call me the queen of social media! And by "they," I mean me and sometimes my friends, but I am confident that more people are going to get the hang of calling me that soon.

The school bus came to a stop, and I walked out into a scene of pandemonium. Everybody was super excited to see one another after the summer. I spotted Sierra and our friend MacKenzie and ran up to them.

"Yay, carrot shirt!" MacKenzie said. "I voted for that one."

"Well, I voted for the purple-and-red minidress," Sierra said. "But you look adorable in this."

"Thanks!" I replied, and then I eyed Sierra's look, a pleated gray-and-black skirt that fell just above her knees and a short-sleeved red sweater. Her thick, curly hair was pulled back with a black headband. "You look fabulous, Si. I need to do a blog post about fall fashion with you."

Then I looked at MacKenzie, comfortable in skinny jeans and a green T-shirt with a rainbow across the front.

"You, too, Kenz," I offered.

MacKenzie laughed. "No thanks, Tamiko. I'm not into fashion like you two are."

"But I need a red-haired model," I said. "Hashtag gingercutie."

"That sounds awful," MacKenzie teased.

"One of these days," I said, and then we made our way into the building.

I found my locker and then headed to my first class, Spanish. As I made my way through the halls, I got stopped by a few kids, most of them complimenting my outfit.

"I read every single blog post you put out this summer," my friend Kyra told me. "Tokyo looks like an amazing city. I hope I can go there someday."

"It's a long plane trip, but totally worth it," I told her.

It was really cool to know that I still had so many

blog readers. I mean, I always got a count of who was reading my posts, but to get feedback from fans in person felt great—kind of like I was a celebrity!

Finally, I got to Spanish class, and there stood Ewan! He smiled, accenting the dimple in his left cheek.

"Hey, it's the world traveler," he said.

"Hey, it's the guy who was stuck in Bayville all summer," I replied.

Ewan laughed. He gets my humor. "It wasn't so bad. You know, people come from hours away to spend the summer in Bayville. The beach is great."

"This is true," I agreed. "Hey, let me see your schedule."

Ewan showed it to me, and I frowned. "This is the only class we have together!"

"Really? That's disappointing," he said. "But at least we . . ."

"!Hola, estudiantes!"

A woman with short, black hair walked into the room.

"Yo soy Señora Hernandez," she said. "In this class we will be seated alphabetically. *So escuchame, por favor.* I will call out your names. Leesa Allan, please take your seat here in the front row. . . ."

I looked at Ewan and frowned. "You're a K, and I'm an S, so . . ."

"See you at lunch, I guess," he said.

Señora Hernandez is one of those people with a lot of energy, and class was very intense, in my opinion, for the first day of school. She even gave us homework!

The rest of my teachers that day were a little more relaxed, and the day went pretty smoothly. That was a little disappointing, actually, because I was hoping for something exciting I could write about in my blog. *Food fight in the cafeteria! Gym class confessions! Teacher who wears crazy ties!* But everyone behaved themselves at lunchtime, we didn't even suit up for gym, and only one of my teachers wore a tie: Mr. Miller, my third-period English teacher, and his was a very tasteful navy tie with black pinstripes. Nothing to blog about there.

The highlight of my day was science class with Sierra, my last class of the day. The teacher was a guy about my dad's age, with dark black hair and a mustache that was actually a pretty cool-looking mustache, not a creepy one.

"I'm Mr. Olabarietta, but everyone calls me

Mr. O.," he began. "Please take a seat where you feel comfortable."

I looked at Sierra and beamed. We could sit together! Some boys got the best seats in the back row, but we found two seats next to each other right in the middle of the classroom.

"We've got a lot of exciting topics coming up this year," Mr. O. continued, "but I like to begin the first day of school by getting to know you. Please introduce yourselves by name and tell me what your animal mascot is."

"What if we don't have a pet?" somebody asked.

Mr. O. shook his head. "No, I mean an animal that you relate to, that you feel shares some of your personality traits," he explained. "For example, my animal mascot is a cheetah, because I like to run. Now, who wants to go first?"

There was an awkward moment as just about everybody stared down at their desk, hoping they wouldn't be called—including me. I know I can be outgoing at times, and I like getting attention on my blog, but Allie recently explained to me that I am what is known as an ambivert—someone who is half introverted and half extroverted. The introverted part of me can spend hours and even days happily by myself, creating things. And sometimes I can get shy.

Sierra, however, is a true extrovert, and she raised her hand.

"My name is Sierra Perez, and my animal mascot is a cat—not a big cat, like a cheetah, but a house cat," she said.

"And why is that?" Mr. O. asked.

"I have this new kitten, Marshmallow, and she's so curious and excited about everything," Sierra said. "And that's just like me!"

You know when they say a person's smile lights up a room? That's Sierra. She beamed when she was talking about her kitten, charming everybody. It's like this special magic that she has.

The extrovert in me wanted to get in on some of that magic, so I raised my hand.

"My name is Tamiko Sato, and my animal mascot is also a cat," I said.

"Why?" Mr. O. asked. "Do you also have an adorable kitten at home?"

"No, it's because I rule over my house, I never obey commands, and I love treats," I said, and everyone in class laughed—including Mr. O. I'd nailed it!

"Well, I did not expect that," he said, wiping his eyes. "I think we found our class clown."

"I'm not a class clown," I replied. "I have a much better fashion sense than that. But you can call me class queen."

"Hmm. I think there's only room in this class for one monarch, and that's me," Mr. O. teased. "Okay, who wants to follow that?"

I smiled. I liked my classes, I liked my teachers, and everyone thought I was funny. A thought popped into my head.

I can feel it. This year I am going to rule the school!

I caught up with Sierra in the hallway after class.

"How'd the rest of your day go?" I asked.

"Not bad," she replied. "But I have Mr. Rivera for art. Now I know what you were complaining about all last year. The way he described the projects we'd be working on almost put me to sleep!"

I nodded. "It's not easy. But if I could get through it, you will!"

Sierra sighed. "Other than that, I got a ton of homework assigned. Can you believe that? Who gives homework on the first day of school?"

"In this, you are not alone," I told her. "I've got a ton to do when I get home."

“Then it’s a good thing you finished your submission for the *Bayville Monthly* magazine cover contest,” Sierra said.

I stopped. “Wait, what?” I asked. “I thought that was next week.”

Sierra looked at her phone. “Nope. You’ve got to get the digital file in by midnight tonight. You asked me to put an alert in my phone because you said you wouldn’t remember. Remember?”

I hugged her. “What would I do without you?” I asked. “When I become a famous fashion executive, will you be my personal secretary?”

“Hmm, Tamiko, that’s not exactly the dream career I imagined,” Sierra replied.

“Well, anyway, thank you!” I said. “I am a genius for asking you to remind me.”

“Or am I a genius for knowing how to use a basic calendar app?” Sierra asked, in what I thought might have been a teensy dig, but I couldn’t tell from the tone of her voice. Anyway, I couldn’t stick around to find out.

“See you tomorrow, Si!” I said, and I ran to catch my bus.

When I got home, I let myself in with my key because there was no sign of Kai yet, and I knew Mom and Dad didn't get back from the college until six on Mondays. Luckily, they'd decided I was mature enough to stay home by myself for a few hours.

I rushed up to my room to finish the art submission that Sierra had reminded me about. I dumped my backpack on my bed and headed into the little side room attached to my bedroom. We live in an old house, and Mom says the little room might have been some kind of baby nursery when the house was built. But with lots of windows letting in bright light, it made the perfect customization space for me.

Some people might call it a "craft room," but I prefer to call it a customization space, because I am not making macaroni picture frames like some kind of summer camper. I am creating and customizing things—like, I'll turn a torn pair of jeans into a cute denim purse, or I'll decoupage a lampshade with pages from manga to decorate my bedroom with.

The customization room is turquoise with white trim, and all my tools and materials are stored in jars and plastic bins. My main workspace is a big metal folding table that I picked up from the curb. It holds my grandma's vintage sewing machine and still leaves room for me to create.

Right now the table was covered with stuff I was using for my art submission. The *Bayville Monthly* was a magazine that talked about all the things to do and places to go in our little beach town. When tourists come to visit, they use it as a guidebook, and any businesses featured in it usually get more traffic.

Every year they hold the Bayville County Youth Arts Contest, where they invited artists up to age eighteen to submit art about their favorite thing about Bayville. I figured that a lot of people would be submitting photos, or drawing pictures of typical stuff, like ocean waves or the boardwalk. But lately I'd been working in collage art, and as the (unofficial) social media director of Molly's Ice Cream, I knew how amazing it would be to get the ice cream shop on the cover.

So I'd started making a Molly's Ice Cream–themed collage. First I'd printed out some of my favorite photos: the vintage metal letters that spelled out "ice cream" that hung on the wall, a jar of rainbow sprinkles, Allie's little brother eating an ice cream cone. Then I'd collected paper stuff from the shop, like a napkin with the shop logo and one of the paper menus that we keep by the register. I'd started arranging them all on a piece of cardstock, and then to fill in the gaps I'd searched through my supplies to find some fun additions. A scrap of fabric with rainbow-colored polka dots reminded me of the sprinkles, glitter cardstock added some sparkle, and cut-out pictures of ice cream from some old kiddie magazines from Japan looked really cute.

Sometimes I just put the images together and—*bam!*—I'm done. But I'd agonized over this piece, moving things around again and again. Now I had to finish it.

I picked up my glue stick, took a deep breath, and attached the first image to the cardstock. I kept going, tweaking my arrangement as I went, and using liquid glue for the fabric. When I was done, I stepped back and held it up.

"Cute," I said. "But it needs something."

Then I spied some glittery pom-poms in one of my bins.

Perfect! I thought. They'll give it some dimension! But I didn't want to go overboard, so I carefully plucked out a few black ones and some white ones, to match the ice cream shop's black-and-white checker-board floor.

When I glued on the last pom-pom, I grinned. The whole thing just looked right. Next I placed the image in a special photo box I made with a white bottom and walls, which I use to photograph stuff for my blog. It helps you get a clean, perfect image without any weird shadows.

I took a few pictures on my phone, chose the best one, and then went to the magazine's website. I filled out the online form and uploaded the photo with the caption: *I ❤ Molly's!*

Then I texted the image to Allie and Sierra.

What do you think? 7 hours before the deadline, Si!

Allie replied first. I love this! I'm going to show it to my mom as soon as she gets home!

I texted her back. Tx. How was your first day at the luxury spa known as Vista Green?

I was teasing Allie about her school. She, Sierra, and I had all gone to the same elementary school together, which is how we became besties. But then Allie's parents had split up, and Allie had moved to a different part of Bayville (the part where the summer people have their mansions, but Allie and her mom and brother live in a tiny apartment there). That's why Allie goes to Vista Green instead of MLK with Sierra and me, and everyone knows that Vista Green has much better equipment and cafeteria food. I think it bugs Allie when we tease her about it, but sometimes I can't resist.

LOL! She replied. Lots of classes with my friends. ☺

You mean your other friends, I teased. Seriously, tho, that's nice. Homework?

Nope, she replied. We had getting-to-know-you games all day, and pizza.

😮🍕!!!! I typed back. No work, no homework, and pizza on top of it! It was hard not to be jealous of the Vista Greenies sometimes.

Sierra chimed in. Your cover looks great, Tamiko!

I was typing a response to her when I heard the front door open.

"Tamiko, we're home!" Mom yelled up the stairs. "Come on down and tell us about how your first day of school went."